Daffodil Dreams

An Appalachia-Inspired Short Story Collection

Daffodil Dreams
An Appalachia-Inspired Short Story Collection

Published June 2022
Mountain Girl Press
Imprint of Jan-Carol Publishing, Inc.

Front Cover Design: Tara Sizemore
Cover Photo: Ilona / Adobe Stock

ISBN: 978-1-954978-54-6
Library of Congress Control Number: 2022941817

This is a work of fiction. Any resemblance to actual persons, either living or dead, is entirely coincidental. All names, characters, and events are the product of the author's imagination.

Jan-Carol Publishing, Inc.
PO Box 701
Johnson City, TN 37605
publisher@jancarolpublishing.com
www.jancarolpublishing.com

This is dedicated to all the talented authors for their participation in this collection of short stories, and to all the readers of Jan-Carol Publishing's books.

Table of Contents

Daffodil Dreams

Dreams of Being a Teacher

Jan Howery

Mary Jane sat nervously in her chair on her high school auditorium stage. It was Saturday, May 10, and graduation day for the Chestnut High School class of 1947. The announcement of the recipient for the only full college scholarship was about to be revealed. Mary Jane was the valedictorian of her class, served on the debate team and on the high school yearbook design committee, and was chosen as the 'best all around' superlative of the senior class. She knew that this college scholarship was her only hope of going to college and fulfilling her dreams of being a teacher.

Mary Jane Blackford was a petite, feisty young lady. She earned her education, without much family encouragement, by walking a mile one way to and from a one room schoolhouse, and many times in the cold, snow, and bad weather. She rode her horse, Blue, to school when the horse was not needed for the farm chores. By the time Mary Jane was entering the seventh grade, the community had grown and built a public-school for grades first through seven, and then a high school building for grades eight through twelve.

Mary Jane's father, James, was a dedicated dairy farmer. He and Mary Jane's mother, Martha, were married at the age of sixteen and set up housekeeping on five acres that were given to them as a wedding gift. Mr. Blackford sold timber to purchase more acres, and he developed a small and family supporting dairy farm. He was known in the community as the 'peddler' or 'wagon merchant' because he would load his wagon with eggs, milk, butter and cheese and garden grown vegetables, and travel from house to house selling his goods.

Mary Jane was the youngest girl of five children. Her older brother was serving in the military. Both her sisters had dropped out of school to help on the farm and were now married with children. Both sisters' husbands helped on the farm. Mary Jane's younger brother was set to graduate from high school the following year after her.

"May I have your attention?" the school principal, Mr. Gentry, asked as he stood on stage and prepared to make the announcement. "The school board and I had a tough decision...with all these well deserving students, we wish we could've awarded each and every one a scholarship. Unfortunately, only one student can be selected. The lucky and well-deserving recipient of this full scholarship is..." Mr. Gentry slowly opened the envelope and read the name, "Sally Ball. Let's give a round of applause for this young lady and the recipient of this fine award!"

The student class gasped, and a small round of applause could be heard from the student body. *She is the salutatorian, and I'm the valedictorian!* Mary Jane thought. *NO! NO! NO! I need this scholarship. I'm smarter! My grades are better! Please...no!*

"Would the Valedictorian and Salutatorian, please stand. Lead the class of 1947 into their future," Mr. Gentry instructed and motioned them stand and exit the stage as the fellow classmates followed.

Mary Jane was numb with shock. She stared ahead and did not make eye contact with anyone. Students called her name, but she ignored them and quickly marched down the aisle to the double doors which led to a large lobby, and from there, quickly made her way out the front doors of the schoolhouse. She ran as fast as she could to her parent's old farm truck and she jumped inside. She tried to keep the tears from falling, but she couldn't. She cried and yelled to the top of her lungs, "Why?" She saw her parents walking toward the truck and tried to compose herself. She didn't want them to know just how much the scholarship had meant to her.

Her father was holding his one and only, worn, 'go to church' fedora hat in one hand and with the other hand opened the truck door for her mother.

"I see it in your eyes," her mother said as she climbed into the truck. "I know you're disappointed."

Mary Jane didn't answer.

"I believe I saw Mr. Hess. I need to ask him about that bull he's got for sale," Mr. Blackford said, and closed the truck door.

Mr. Blackford walked back to the auditorium and saw Mr. Gentry on the stage stacking chairs. "Mr. Gentry...may I have a word with you?" Mr. Blackford asked.

"What's on your mind?" Mr. Gentry asked coldly without looking at Mr. Blackford.

"I...I...I wanted to ask you about that scholarship," Mr. Blackford stammered.

"The decision is final," Mr. Gentry answered as he continued to stack the chairs.

"I understand," Mr. Blackford said softly. "But could you tell me how the decision was made? My girl...she's smart...and she's worked hard. I mean...I don't have a lot of book learning, but she does. She's awfully upset."

Mr. Gentry took a deep breath and looked Mr. Blackford in the eyes. "You are a successful farmer, aren't you, Mr. Blackford?"

"I do okay," Mr. Blackford replied.

"You turned 300 acres into a workable farm, and it provides for you and your family, right?" Mr. Gentry asked.

"Well...yes."

"I doubt that you'll be sending your daughter on to college...she is needed on the farm," Mr. Gentry said and before Mr. Blackford could respond, Mr. Gentry continued, "Do you know Mr. Ball? Sally's father?"

"I know of him, like everyone else 'round here," Mr. Blackford answered confidentially.

"Then, you're aware that he owns a couple of small coal mining operations?" Mr. Gentry asked.

"Yes," Mr. Blackford replied.

"You see, Mr. Blackford, you have a producing farm...you and your family. You work together on that farm. You need to work together for your farm to continue. You and your children and your children's children must work together for the future of that farm. Don't you agree?" Mr. Gentry asked directly.

"Yes, but...," Mr. Blackford tried to answer, but was interrupted.

"Mr. Ball has two children, a boy and a girl. The boy is positioned to take over his father's coal mining operations, but his girl is not. Therefore, she will go to college, use her education as a career for herself, and be a part of our growing community; whereas, your daughter, Mr. Blackford, has a choice. She could go on to college and return back to the community, but will she continue on the farm, or want a career in our community? She has a choice. Sally did not," Mr. Gentry said. "So, the board and I decided that Sally should be awarded the scholarship because we believe that she is more likely use that scholarship for the purpose of the scholarship...to secure a future."

"But Mr. Ball can afford to send his girl to college. I...we...don't have the money to send our girl to college. It doesn't seem fair. Her grades were the best!" Mr. Blackford pleated. "Without that scholarship, you just decided her future for her and you just took her choices away! You're leaving her no choice."

"I am sorry, Mr. Blackford," Mr. Gentry said. "The choice...our decision is final." Mr. Gentry returned to stacking chairs.

Mr. Blackford placed his hat on his head, turned, and walked back to his truck. As he opened the door of the truck, he looked at Martha and shook his head no. He started up the old farm truck, and no word was spoken as they headed home down the dirt road. When they arrived home, Mary Jane jumped out of the truck and thought, *that was the longest five miles of my life.*

A few hours later, her mother was preparing supper when she heard a knock at the door and peeked out the window. "Mary Jane, Tommy's at the door."

Tommy White was a handsome, uneducated, 20-year-old young man. In his short lifetime, he had seen his share of challenges. His mother, Eunice was only 15 years old when she found herself pregnant. She had shamed herself and her family. At eight months pregnant, she walked to a swinging bridge to jump to her death when a passerby stopped her. But after Tommy was born, her parents kicked her out of the house and refused to allow her to see her son. She moved in with relatives in another state to start a new life. So, Tommy only knew his grandparents as his mother and father.

"Mary Jane, are you going to answer the door? It sounds like Tommy is beating it down!" her mother yelled.

"NO! I'm not seeing anyone!" Mary Jane shouted.

About that time, her mother opened the front door and said, "Tommy, you don't have to beat the door down son. We hear you. Come on in and go sit in the parlor. Mary Jane will be down directly."

Tommy's face turned red, and he gave Martha a weak smile.

Martha walked upstairs to Mary Jane's room and opened the door without knocking. "You're dressed. Go on downstairs and entertain your beau."

"I don't want to see anyone," Mary Jane cried.

"Well, Tommy's here to congratulate you. He's smitten with you. And you *will* go downstairs to see him. Now!" her mother instructed.

Mary Jane followed her mother reluctantly down the stairs and walked into the parlor.

"I heard," Tommy said to Mary Jane as she walked into the parlor.

"Heard what?" Mary Jane asked and sat down.

"You were cheated out of the scholarship you deserved," Tommy answered. "And I can tell that you've been crying. I'm so sorry."

"Well, it's final. And it's done," Mary Jane said bravely.

Her mother stepped inside and asked, "Tommy, are you staying for supper?"

"No," Mary Jane answered at the same time that Tommy answered, "Yes."

"Tommy, you're welcomed to stay for supper, and I've set a place for you. Supper's ready."

After supper, Tommy and Mary Jane sat on the front porch swing, but Mary Jane didn't have much to say. Tommy just enjoyed being near her, even if it meant sitting in silence.

From inside the house, Mary Jane's father yelled, "Tommy, it's getting dark and you've got a mile to walk home, boy. Don't you think you should be going on?"

"Yes, sir," Tommy quickly replied and stood. "You going to be at church tomorrow?" he asked Mary Jane.

"I guess so. I'll see you tomorrow," Mary Jane replied.

* * *

Two weeks had gone by and no one talked about the scholarship. Mary Jane seemed to go through the motions and do her chores aimlessly.

"Mary Jane, after we clean up the dishes from supper, you and I are going to have a talk," her mother instructed Mary Jane.

"About what?" Mary Jane asked.

Her mother never answered her. Her father took his evening coffee and went to sit on the front porch swing. After the clean-up was complete, her mother motioned to Mary Jane to go to the parlor.

"What's wrong Mother?" Mary Jane asked as they walked into the parlor.

"What's wrong? Everything!" her mother answered and sat down. "You've been dragging 'round for the last two weeks like you lost your best friend."

Mary Jane just stared at her with no reply.

"Mary Jane, of all my young'uns, you've been the one who always gave honor to me and your pa. You never back talked us, did what you were told, did your chores, and you always made us proud. We're still proud of you, but...now...you're a young woman. You're older than I was when I got married. You're older than when you sisters got married. It's time for you to move out...and move on with your life."

"What? I don't understand," Mary Jane said. "I can go to college?"

"No. You need a husband. Your pa and I cannot afford to send you away to college, so the choice left for you is to get married and have a family...your family," her mother said firmly.

"A husband?" Mary Jane gasped.

"Yes. Now, let's see. Which one? You've been sparkin' with Dewey Sims and Tommy White. Which one do you like best?" her mother asked.

"As a husband? Neither," Mary Jane snapped.

"Let me see. Tommy has a bad reputation. You know that he's a bastard, and it's told that he's lazy. What about Dewey?" her mother asked.

"Dewey? Oh yes. I can be the queen of the moonshine still over the hill!" Mary Jane said sarcastically.

"Yes. Dewey and his family have a couple of illegal moonshine stills. But they do well with 'em," her mother snickered.

"But he always has stinky breath from alcohol. I think he drinks too much," Mary Jane said seriously.

"This is true. Nothing's worse than an alcoholic husband. Your sister's dealing with that mess now and it can cause a lot of problems," her mother said. "But Tommy's got a reputation of bein' lazy."

"I don't think he's lazy. Just uneducated. He can't find a job because of the lack of education," Mary Jane said sympathetically.

"Is there anyone else?" her mother asked.

Mary Jane shook her head.

"Then the choice is made. It's Tommy as my son-in-law," her mother confirmed.

"I don't love him," Mary Jane said.

"You don't have to, and you'll learn to love him," her mother said. "I'll have pa talk to him about asking you to marry him and we'll have a June wedding. We'll set it for June 30th. That'll give us time for planning. The house that your sister and husband moved out of when they moved in with her in-laws is empty and a good place. It'll be the wedding gift. Just a half mile away. A house with five acres is a good start. But we'll have to get Tommy a job. Probably here on the farm. It's done."

Mary Jane just stared at her mother. *She's serious,* she thought.

"Mother, is that all there is for me...my future?" Mary Jane asked. "I always had dreams of being a teacher."

"Your husband, Tommy, will be your first student. And you'll have a family," her mother answered, stood up, and walked out to the front porch to sit next to James.

Mary Jane sat in the parlor in silence. She thought, *my life but not my choices. I guess this is my future.*

Ten years later...

Mary Jane and Tommy had two children, a boy, David, and a girl, Jan. Tommy provided well for his family and found a good job as a bulldozer operator and Foreman for a small coal mining operation until retirement. He farmed the wedding gift of the five acres, bought more property, and built a small farm of one hundred acres that helped support the family needs. Mary Jane worked as a stay-at-home mom and managed the household.

It was warm sunny July Sunday morning when Tommy, Mary Jane, and their children entered the small country church and Mary Jane was asked to serve as a substitute for the Sunday School teacher who became sick and had to leave. Mary Jane gladly accepted.

It was on the fourth Sunday that Mary Jane was approached after service by the Preacher. "Mrs. White, the Deacons of the church and I would like to meet with you."

"Certainly," Mary Jane replied. "Tommy, take the kids to the car and I will see you shortly."

Mary Jane walked to the front of the little church and sat down in the first pew. The Preacher stood at the pulpit and the deacons sat where the choir usually sat.

"Mrs. White, I'm sure that you are aware that our former Sunday School teacher will not be returning due to her illness, and we are now in a position to hire someone permanent," the Preacher said.

"Yes," Mary Jane answered.

"Well, we know that you've been serving as a substitute for her, and you've taught for a month of Sundays now. All of us as church leaders must follow the good book in our leadership in church for our congregation. We follow; no drinking, no dancing, women do not wear men's clothes, and...women don't wear makeup and...women do not color their hair."

Mary Jane gasped.

"Mrs. White, do you color your hair?" the Preacher asked sternly.

"Well...I do. I'm going gray, prematurely, I think. So, I..." Mary Jane tried to explain, but was interrupted.

"I'm sure you understand. We've decided to hire Anna Rose Bostice to replace our Sunday School teacher. You are not legible," the preacher said coldly.

"But..." Mary Jane was interrupted again.

"Would you consider not coloring your hair?" the preacher asked harshly.

Mary Jane was so embarrassed. She felt the tears rise in her eyes.

"Our decision is final. You cannot teach our Sunday School class," the Preacher said with amens sounding from the deacons.

Mary Jane stood, walked out the church doors, and choked back her tears. *I can't teach. Why? All I ever dreamed of was being a teacher*, she thought as she opened the car door and hopped inside.

"What happened?" Tommy asked. "You look like you've seen a ghost."

"I guess I did," Mary Jane answered. "I was told that because I color my hair, I'm not worthy to teach... teach...the Sunday School class."

Tommy angrily replied, "What? Ol' man Preacher Stevens wears that bird's nest, rat chewed, chicken shit toupee to church every Sunday, and he thinks that God doesn't see that as a sin? I'll just go in and take it off his head and put it up his..."

Laughing between tears, Mary Jane interrupted Tommy. "Tommy! The kids!"

"Well, that's a shame!" Tommy said sympathetically and calmed down.

"It's final. The decision is final," Mary Jane said quietly.

"We'll find another church. We don't have to attend here. It'll be okay. So...why don't we go on out to town and get some ice cream?" Tommy asked. "It'll cheer ya up."

Mary Jane smiled and nodded yes.

A lifetime later...

Tommy died of lung disease from working in the coal industry. Mary Jane continued to be a stay-at-home mom, raised her family, and provided care for her parents until they passed. But a couple years after Tommy passed, Mary Jane showed evidence of the progressive dementia disease. Jan and her brother decided to place Mary Jane in an assisted living for daily care.

It was a spring day in May when Jan got the dreaded phone call. It was Mary Jane's doctor, and he indicated that he wasn't sure Mary Jane would last through the end of the day. Mary Jane's time was nearing.

"Mom...mom...do you know who I am?" Mary Jane's daughter, Jan, asked as she took her mother's hand and looked into her eyes.

"Where am I?" Mary Jane asked in a whisper.

"We talked about this mom. You're in this wonderful home away from home. Remember?" Jan asked.

"Where's Tommy?" Mary Jane asked with wide opened eyes and appeared scared.

"Remember, Mom. He's gone. He's singing with the angels now," Jan answered. "He's been singing with the angels for a few years now."

"I'm going to join him and help him sing with the angels," Mary Jane replied softly. Then as if reality snapped in, Mary Jane looked at her daughter and said very sadly, "I always had dreams of being a teacher."

"You are!" Jan answered enthusiastically.

"I am?" Mary Jane asked with her eyes wide open again. "I am a teacher!?"

"Yes! Yes, you are! You are the best teacher any daughter could ever have!"

Mary Jane grinned real big and, as she closed her eyes for the last time, she softly said, "I am a teacher."

Finally...

Lori C. Byington

One early morning on Tuesday, May 29, 1945, two fat robins hopped daintily along the window ledge and picked at leftover sunflower seeds that had been strewn earlier. Lorrine eyed the pair dreamily. The male robin was bright red with his tuft of feathers perched proudly as he strutted in an attempt to attract the muted-red female robin. She was paying no mind. Lorrine chuckled.

"I wonder when Charlie will be home?" She said aloud and sighed heavily. "V-E Day was three weeks ago. Where is my Sweetie?"

"Is Daddy coming today?" Roxie asked excitedly as she skipped down the hall to the kitchen, as the smell of bacon, toast, and eggs wafted to the ceiling. Her brown curls bounced in time with her skips, and she had her math and history books in her arms. "That smells good, Mother! I am hungry," she said as she plopped down at the round kitchen table snugged in the corner beside the stove.

Lorrine tried to sound brave and put on a strong façade. "I don't know for sure, Roxie. All I know is what I get from letters and phone calls from Elizabeth. She is still in London helping her Women's Army Corp crew dismantle the offices and store the flak books and maps," she answered her inquisitive daughter.

Lorrine wrinkled her brow and jabbed a fork at the bacon that sizzled in the Lodge cast iron pan. Hot bacon grease popped out and several drops splattered onto Lorrine's skin. She jumped and grabbed her hand, which sent the fork flying over her right shoulder and onto the floor. "Son of a buck," she yelled as she clutched her hand. The sting of the grease was not as hurtful as the sting of missing her husband.

"Are you alright, Mother?" Roxie asked worriedly as she rose to help. "I'll get some butter for the burn."

"I am fine, Roxie. Just a few drops hit," Lorrine whispered. Tears started to form in her blue eyes, but she quickly stopped them. She had to put on a brave front for her daughter.

"Hellooooo!" a familiar voice trilled from the living room. The front door closed with a thud, and Roxie closed the refrigerator door and looked up quizzically. When the voice and body entered the kitchen Roxie yelled, "Aunt Earlie! I am so glad you are here! Mother got burned by bacon grease and won't let me help."

"Oh, Earlie, I am fine," Lorrine sighed. "Just a few drops...nothing to worry about." Lorrine glanced at the black and white cat clock on the wall. The tail swung in time to the seconds, which added whimsy to the place. "Gracious, Roxie. You need to get to school. Fourth grade is nothing to take lightly," Lorrine urged as she dabbed the top of her hand with a muted green kitchen towel. "Now, get your books and we will get to Anderson Street School before you are late! Oh dear, take the bacon and toast with you to eat on the way."

As Lorrine and Roxie started to the front door, Lorrine said over her shoulder, "Earlie, I am going on to the draft board after I drop Roxie off. We are getting some boys home, and I want to be there."

"No bother, dear. I will clean up the kitchen and tidy the house a bit," Earlie said comfortingly. "I will listen to W.O.P.I on the radio a bit, too. To hear if any news is good, you know."

Lorrine knew exactly what Aunt Earlie was talking about. Lorrine swathed her silk, yellow scarf around her head and tied a knot under her chin and, once again, stalled stubborn tears.

After she dropped off Roxie at school just in time, Lorrine steered her green Dodge station wagon off Anderson Street and headed to Shelby Street to the Tennessee Post Office, where her office was on the third floor. Once parked, she adjusted her scarf around her perfectly coifed bouffant and stepped out of the car. Lorrine's attitude and demeanor changed as soon as she shut the car door. She glanced up at the window that was her office and swore she saw a figure in Navy dress. Lorrine shook her head, steadied herself and switched on an all business mentality and façade. The soldiers who were coming home must be met by someone who was stable and compassionate.

I wish Charlie were in this group, she thought wistfully, but she knew there was no word from the Edward L. Doheny, the ship in the Pacific on which her husband was commissioned. Lorrine trudged up the two black, marble staircases to her office where the names and records of all men who had gone to war were safely kept. She opened the door and glanced at the polished brass plaque that greeted anyone who was "called up" to serve his country:

Selective Service
Board #103
Mrs. Grace Lorrine W. Woolsy

She sighed and made her way to her walnut desk, which had neat stacks of files of the boys who were to arrive in a bit. "Well, I know the families will be so happy to see their men home," she said aloud.

Lorrine sat down and began to filter through her piles of paperwork. As an afterthought, she turned on her Philco radio to W.O.P.I. to hear any news of, really, anything. A loud crackle and squawk met her ears when she turned the off/on dial to the right. She adjusted the bandwidth dial until she heard the familiar voice of Bill Wilson, the on-duty host.

"Ladies and gentlemen in my listening area, today the President of the United States, Harry S. Truman, announced most ceremoniously that all servicemen and women would be returning to their homes as soon as possible. With the end of the war in our rearview mirror, we can look forward to familiar faces and peaceful times once again. Both Bristol mayors have announced a tentative welcome home ticker-tape parade that will venture down State Street starting at the Bristol Train Station, march through the Bristol "Good Place to Live" sign, and continue on to the end of State Street where a stage will be set up to welcome our men and women home again. A formal date will be announced from this station as soon as possible. Signing off for now....Bill Wilson."

Lorrine turned around in her chair to look out the window onto Sixth Street and let out her breath in a whoosh. She must have been holding her breath because her heart was pounding in her chest. She put her right hand over her heart and breathed in through pursed lips. Tears started to form in her eyes, so she quickly wiped the wetness away with the back of her hand.

A quiet "Ahem..." sounded behind Lorrine's back, and she spun around in her chair to see a haggard but clean shaven face. The fellow immediately took of his Naval blue garrison cap and nodded his head at Lorrine.

"I know I am a bit early, but I wanted to get a jump on signing my papers so I can go see my family," the lieutenant said sheepishly. "I hope I am not bothering you."

Lorrine cleared her throat before she answered. The Naval cap had startled her and made her heart jump. *Silly me,* she thought. *Charlie is not as short as this Navy man.*

"Of course, you are not bothering me," she smiled and said as she removed her yellow scarf. She waved her left hand in a circular motion as an indication for the lieutenant to sit in one of the sturdy gray, government-issued metal chairs. At least the chairs had cushions. "Now, who are you and from where did you decommission?"

"Harlan Dunn," the Navy man answered with pride.

Lorrine continued to smile and began shuffling through the fifty or so files on her desk.

The lieutenant continued, "I served on the U.S.S. Swanson DD-443. She was Gleaves Class Destroyer, you know. She was something else!" The fellow had a gleam in his eye when he talked about the ship. "She was decommissioned a few weeks ago, and I disembarked in San Diego. I sure had a long trip back here to Bristol. I thought I would never get off a darned train."

Lorrine admired his exuberance and pride. "I found your file, Lieutenant Dunn. Just sign a few papers I have marked for you and you can be on your way," she said as she handed the file to the Navy man. The lieutenant grinned from ear to ear when he took the file and began to sign on the dotted lines. Before he left, the Navy man stood and made a short bow to Lorrine.

"Thank ye muchly Mrs. Woolsy. You have a hard job, but no one can tell. At least I could not. God bless and thanks again," the fellow offered.

Lorrine rose from her chair and stood straight as an arrow behind her desk.

"Well, you are welcome lieutenant. We all are doing our part during this war. I am so glad you are home safely," she said. She hoped the lieutenant did not notice the tears hidden in her blue eyes.

Throughout the day other men came back from various locations they had been during World War II. All strode into Lorrine's office with a tired but determined look of relief. When the last file was neatly placed in the drawer on the left of her walnut desk, she started to close the drawer. She slowly drew her finger along the label marked "Home" and took a deep breath. *When will your papers be signed, Charlie?* she thought wistfully.

Lorrine peeked at the large, black clock ticking on the wall above her door. The little hand was on the three and the big hand was on the four.

"Son of a buck! I will be late to pick up Roxie from school!" Lorrine yelled out loud. She grabbed her brown, leather purse, put her yellow scarf around her hair, tied it below her chin and dashed out the office door. She waved at the others who had offices on the third floor of the Bristol, Tennessee Post Office and scampered down the flights of marble stairs. Her heels clacked like a horse clopping down cobblestones.

* * *

Roxie, brown curls bouncing, skittered out of the front door of Anderson Street School and jumped into the open passenger door of the station wagon. "Guess what!" she gushed, blue eyes bright.

"Well, I don't know. Let me try," Lorrine said and grinned at her effusive daughter.

She thought for a moment and tried to remember what Roxie would have done in school that day. The morning seemed a long, long time ago.

"You made an A on your math test!" Lorrine deduced.

Roxie rolled her eyes, snorted and responded a bit haughtily, "Well, of course I made an A on my math test! No...guess again."

Lorrine pursed her lips and thought silently a moment.

"Well? Give up?" Roxie asked a bit impatiently. Before Lorrine could answer her daughter, Roxie offered, "We got to listen on W.O.P.I radio to President Truman! He talked about real things going on today. He said the Marines did something in Japan, but I don't remember what, but he said *all* servicemen were on their way home, if they were not home already! Daddy is on his way home!"

Lorrine's throat clenched and realized Roxie emphasized *all* servicemen. She could not hold back the tears anymore.

Roxie stopped mid-sentence and looked worriedly at her mother. "Mother, what is wrong? What did I say? Is the news not great?"

Lorrine composed herself then, which was something she had done the day Charlie left for sea. She had to be strong for Roxie. But this day, with men coming home and being reunited with families, emotion had caught up with Lorrine's stone-faced demeanor. She dabbed her eyes with her white handkerchief and began hesitantly,

"Roxie, I got notice that your daddy had disembarked the Doheny, but that was three weeks ago. I don't know where he is, and cousin Elizabeth has no news since she is still with the WACs in London. I didn't know how to tell you. I am so sorry!"

Roxie stared at her mother fiercely but quickly smiled. "So!? President Truman said all men were on the way home, and I know Daddy is too!" she said matter-of-factly.

Lorrine just smiled at her strong daughter and put the Dodge in gear to go home. For some reason, the gear shift went into R and the car lurched backwards with an awful jerk.

"Mother! Stop!!" yelled Roxie.

Lorrine blinked and stated, "Well, that has never happened before." She calmly put the car into D and started home. Roxie rolled her eyes and crossed her arms.

The ladies soon arrived at their house on Windsor Avenue, and after several tries, Lorrine *finally* parallel parked in front. Roxie jumped impatiently out of the car door and bounded up the steps and into the front door.

"Aunt Earlie! Aunt Earlie!" She yelled as she pushed open the heavy, oak door.

Earlie walked from the kitchen into the parlor engulfed by her white apron with strawberries on it, holding an olive-green dish towel in her hands.

"Gracious young 'un. What's all the commotion about?" she asked as she pushed back a strand of gray hair that had escaped the neat bun on the top of her head.

Roxie was bursting her buttons with excitement and started rambling, "We heard President Truman on W.O.P.I. on the radio at school today! He promised all Army, Navy, Air Force, Marines and WAC's who had been overseas for the War were coming home soon! Daddy will be home! I just know it!"

Just as Roxie finished her big news, Lorrine walked slowly into the parlor. "I heard the news too, Earlie, on W.O.P.I. earlier today," she nodded in agreement.

Earlie grinned and winked, "I heard the same here while I was thawing the cubed steak for dinner. Mr. Wilson sure sounds official, doesn't he? I wonder where he gets *his* news."

Lorrine walked hurriedly to the coat rack in the corner and hung up her light, tan rain coat along with her yellow head scarf. She hesitated before she commented more. Her heart was still in her throat with worry, and she did not know how to tell Roxie and Earlie about the constant influx of enthusiastic men who came into the office to be officially discharged. Still no word on Charlie, though.

"Well, I can tell you the offices were humming on the third floor of the Post Office, that is for sure. I couldn't tell what people were saying exactly, but the air was electric with excitement and hope," she offered, her face still slightly pointing toward the coat rack. When she finally turned and looked Earlie in the eyes, Earlie could tell the worry was seeping through every bone in Lorrine's body.

"Well, the steak and gravy aren't going to cook themselves. I better get to peeling potatoes for the masher. Roxie, come help me please. You can open the cans of peas and put the flour into the cup of milk so it can mix to make the gravy," Earlie sort of ordered as she gently tried to get Roxie's mind off her daddy for the moment.

Lorrine nodded to Earlie in agreement and thankfulness. "Roxie, go help Aunt Earlie and then you can do your homework before supper is ready," she said as she shooed her daughter toward the kitchen door.

"Oh...okay, Mother. Mrrmmph...But I wanted to listen to the radio to hear if there is more news of daddy!" Roxie admitted with a huff.

Knowing she needed to mind and help, Roxie drug her nine-and-a-half-year-old feet into the kitchen behind Aunt Earlie. Aunt Earlie held the door for Roxie to go through and turned to glance at Lorrine. Lorrine had already turned toward the front door and was simply staring at nothing, hands clasped tightly in front of her waist. Earlie sighed and left her be as she followed Roxie into the kitchen and let the door swing shut quietly behind her.

After supper, Lorrine and Aunt Earlie were cleaning up the dirty Lodge cast iron pans and Schumann dishes while they listened to Johnny Mercer sing "On the Atchison, Topeka and the Santa Fe" on the radio in the kitchen. Roxie had gone to her room to do her math homework and to read her *Good Times on Our Street* book. Aunt Earlie glanced over at Lorrine, who was drying the supper dishes with a 1944 calendar dish towel. Lorrine's hands were shaking a bit, so Earlie took the dish gently out of Lorrine's hands. Lorrine peered up at Earlie in silence. Held-back too long, tears formed in Lorrine's blue eyes and her nose was about to run. She put the faded dish towel over her face and let the tears fall. Earlie gently put her arms around her niece for comfort, but Earlie knew only a husband's return could fix this hurt.

A few minutes later, Roxie's footsteps thundered down the hall and through the dining room. Lorrine quickly dried her eyes with the dish towel and stepped back from Aunt Earlie. Roxie pushed open the kitchen door, wide-eyed, and exclaimed, "Cousin Elizabeth is on the phone! Didn't you hear the ringing?? Hurry, she is on a coded line from London!"

Lorrine and Earlie looked at each other in shock and bumped into one another as they headed out the kitchen swinging door after Roxie. Roxie reached the phone on the hall shelf on the hallway wall and excitedly told the person on the other end, "Hold on, Elizabeth! Mother is here..."

Lorrine grabbed the phone out of Roxie's hand, and gawked wide-eyed first at Roxie and then at Aunt Earlie, and, shaking, put the ear-piece so all three could hear her cousin on the other end.

"Hello...Elizabeth? This is Lorrine. How are you?"

The line crackled, and Elizabeth sounded like she was in a barrel, but the ladies could hear a voice they had not heard in a year.

"Lorrine! I couldn't get through to Bristol before now, so I am so sorry! London phone and morse code lines have been up and running, but the overflow of calls going in and out of the country is staggering," Elizabeth began. "I mailed a letter three weeks ago, but since I didn't hear back from you, I thought you must not have received it."

Abruptly, loud static started on the phone line, and Elizabeth's voice went in and out of ear shot. Lorrine put the phone closer to her ear and stared helplessly at Roxie and Earlie. All at once, crackling stopped—the line went dead.

All three looked at one another in horror. They faintly heard Johnny Mercer...*I reckon she knows she's gonna meet a friend. Folks around these parts set the time of day. From the Atchison, Topeka and the Santa Fe*....wafting from the radio in the kitchen.

A loud *wham* all of a sudden emanated from around the wall where the women still glared at the phone in Lorrine's hands.

"Sweetie! Sweetie!! I'm home! I smell steak and gravy. Did you get Elizabeth's letter?" resounded from the front door.

The ladies gaped in disbelief, but Roxie yelled, "Daddy, Daddy, you're home! I knew you were coming!" as she scooted around the wall and into her daddy's outstretched arms. Charlie dropped his gear and swept his daughter into the biggest bear hug this side of heaven has ever seen.

"Oh, I missed you "Sweetheart! Where is your mother?" Charlie said happily through teary eyes.

At that moment Lorrine peeped around the corner of the wall and met eyes with her husband, finally home from sea. She started to faint but caught herself as Aunt Earlie helped her to steady. She stood erect, smiled, and started to cry at last.

"Oh Sweetie, Sweetie! You are home! You are home!" Lorrine yelled as she ran into his right arm, while his left arm still held Roxie tight.

The three hugged and cried and hugged harder, and Earlie, who witnessed the long-awaited reunion, smiled wide and wiped big tears from her eyes with the wrinkled, 1944 calendar dish towel.

"Daddy, you are not going away again!" Roxie said matter-of-factly and kissed his cheek. "Mother can take care of a lot, but she needs someone to drive us around. She can't drive well at all!"

First Aid

Lynda A. Holmes

Growing up in north Georgia during the 1950s and 1960s, my family exhibited the hallmarks of Southern Appalachian people: courage and strength with unflinching resilience. I was fortunate to be there to observe and learn from them.

Most folks probably don't keep an apron in their car as part of the first-aid kit.

Back in 1962, my Mama did just that, insisting that her home-sewn, red apron might come in handy. She stashed the first-aid apron under the driver's seat.

Mama explained, "The pockets are perfect for antiseptic and band aids."

The first-aid apron solved various problems. Whenever we needed our car to stand out from others in a crowded parking lot, Mama knew exactly what to do. She just grabbed the first-aid apron, dumped the first-aid supplies on the seat, and tied the bright, red apron onto the antenna.

When Mama's car had a flat tire and she called Daddy for help, someone asked Daddy how he could find us in a crowded parking lot.

Daddy replied, "Simple. It will be the only car flying a red apron from the antenna."

The first-aid apron also served as a blanket or tourniquet when necessary. One summer afternoon, a neighborhood terrier named Copper was injured badly when he fought with a stray dog that wandered onto our road. After the skirmish, the poor creature was barely moving. Mama and I saw everything from our house. No one was home at Copper's house.

"We've got to help Copper," Mama said.

I followed Mama as she went to the car and unwrapped the first-aid apron. We walked over to the victim, cautiously surveying his injuries. Although the animal was breathing, he was bloody and hurt and in need of a vet. Mama opened the first-aid apron, calmly talking to the dog and rolling him into the red fabric. He whimpered pathetically.

Mama picked up the dog, bundled in the first-aid apron, and we walked to the car. I slid onto the front seat, and Mama placed the wrapped dog in my lap.

"Talk softly to him," she directed.

Mama drove to the vet's office as quickly as the speed limit would allow us. Choking back tears, I tried to speak to the dog. He lay very still in my lap. Occasionally, he let out a slight whimper.

After examining the dog, the vet said that Copper should stay there for a while.

Copper's family thanked Mama and me, praising us for volunteering to save the injured dog. Mama shrugged off their praise, saying, "It was the right thing to do, and we did it."

Copper survived, although he moved with a slight limp on one side.

Mama sewed a new red apron for the first-aid kit.

Shortly after the Copper experience, Mama and I were on our way to do the weekly grocery shopping when we saw something ahead in the middle of the road.

Since there were no cars behind us, Mama slowed down.

Stopping the car abruptly, Mama exclaimed, "Little hen, little hen," and clicked on our emergency lights.

A hen and her chicks had picked that moment to march across the highway.

Before the hen and chicks could get across the road, a pick-up truck came barreling along behind us, hardly slowing down at all. The driver lost control of the wheel, side-swiping us as the truck veered off the road into a telephone pole.

Our vehicle was whacked sideways in the road. Mama and I were thrown, whiplash style, forward and then backwards.

Meanwhile, the hen and chicks trekked into the woods on the other side of the road, safe from harm and oblivious to human catastrophe.

"Mama, are you all right?" I sobbed, with tears flooding down my face. Tasting their saltiness, I saw Mama open her eyes. She blinked several times and then sat up straight, gingerly lifting her arms and tilting her neck from one side to the other.

I let out a sigh of relief at Mama's response: "I think I'm okay...will probably be sore tomorrow."

Mama reached out and took my hand, asking, "How are you, dear?"

"I'm...okay," I answered, still sobbing and wiping away my tears.

Mama continued, "We're fortunate to be alive."

"The hen and chicks made it across the road," I said.

"Good, but we've got to help those folks in the truck," Mama replied, opening the car door on her side. She mumbled, "A wreck and a traffic ticket all on the same day, probably."

Mama grabbed the first-aid apron as she slid out of the car, cleaning a scrape on my forehead with the antiseptic. I didn't even realize that I was hurt.

Moving toward the truck, we saw a scary sight–the truck was wrapped around the telephone pole. The driver appeared to be unconscious, his bloody head lying cramped against the steering wheel. His passenger was moaning.

As Mama and I spoke to the conscious passenger, we heard a siren in the distance.

When two cars of policemen arrived, they called an ambulance and questioned us, directing traffic around the scene. Mama told them about stopping to let the hen and chicks cross the road and turning on the emergency blinkers shortly before the truck slammed into us.

Some of the policemen peered under a tarpaulin in the back of the truck with a flashlight.

The ambulance arrived with its siren bawling and flashing, and one of the policemen made an announcement.

"Hopefully both men will survive to face their arrests. The back of the truck is loaded with electrical equipment. I ran the license plate of the truck and it's hot, all right."

Although we didn't know much police lingo, we did know that "hot" meant stolen. Our mouths dropped open as Mama and I looked at each other.

The policeman continued, "We've been hunting these thieves for weeks. You two caught them for us today. We've checked their IDs."

"Ma'am, we need you and your daughter to come back to the police station for a statement."

Mama still clutched the first-aid apron in her hands.

Another vehicle pulled up alongside us. It was from one of our local TV stations. A reporter jumped out with a microphone in her hand, as the cameraman shined a bright light in our faces.

The reporter asked, "Officer, may we have a comment?"

The policeman who was escorting us said, "Miss, this lady here and her daughter helped us solve a crime today. Thanks to them, we've solved the case of the missing electronics that has baffled our community for weeks."

The reporter questioned Mama, "Ma'am, do you work for the police department?"

"Oh, no. My daughter and I were on our way to do some grocery shopping, when a little hen and her chicks marched across the road ..."

Mama related our story and the reporter called her a hero. She questioned Mama about the first-aid apron. Then she asked, "Ma'am, do you have some parting advice for our viewers?"

I studied Mama, predicting what she would say. She answered, "Be prepared to do the right thing, when it is up to you to do it."

The cameraman snapped some photos of Mama and me and the two wrecked vehicles.

We rode in the police car to the station, where Mama phoned Daddy. Relieved that we were unhurt, he picked us up from the police station. Daddy had our car towed to an auto-service center.

That evening, a few minutes into the TV news, there was Mama smiling at the camera. She was holding the first-aid apron with one hand and hugging me with the other.

The reporter ended the interview as she looked straight into the camera and said, "Thanks to all of the everyday heroes who make life better for others in so many ways."

The next day, a photo of Mama and me appeared in our local newspaper, *The County View*, with a caption stating, "Local woman is prepared with First-Aid Apron." Beneath the caption, we read a brief account of yesterday's events.

We were pleased to read that the criminals were recovering at a nearby hospital (handcuffed to their beds, in order to avoid escape).

Mama received calls from people who wanted to be her agents for marketing the first-aid apron. She told them that she would consider it.

At school, my classmates and teachers asked for my autograph beside our picture in the paper. I imagined that the way I felt must be the way that President and Mrs. Kennedy felt if they signed autographs for people visiting the White House.

Our principal asked me to find out whether Mama would consider making a first-aid apron for every grade in the school. She agreed, and in a week or two every grade had its own first-aid apron with pockets full of supplies for emergencies.

Mama taught me well through her actions, the use of her talents, and her words.

To this day, I keep a first-aid apron under the front seat of the family car.

I Swear, Lynn

Linda Hudson Hoagland

"Sam, who does this lipstick belong to?"

"It's yours, isn't it?"

"No. What other woman have you been driving around in this old pickup truck?" asked Lynn as she forced a smile to her lips.

"You're the only one, I swear, Lynn. There has been no other woman in this pickup," answered a flustered Sam.

"Why would this lipstick be in here?" Lynn asked as she pulled the cover off the cylindrical tube so she could see the color that was identified as Mystic Red on the bottom label.

Sam glanced at the red lipstick and immediately turned away to hide the evidence of the creeping, crimson embarrassment that he felt traveling up from his toes to the top of his head.

"This isn't my color. This is a shade some cheap floozy would choose," Lynn said as she tossed it out the truck window.

Sam tried to see where the lipstick landed so he could retrieve it as soon as Lynn wasn't with him in the truck. He wanted to keep it to remind him of where the lipstick came from and why it was there. Someday he might tell Lynn the truth, but not now—maybe not ever—he hoped.

Lynn didn't believe Sam. The evidence was there. She had held it in her hand. He was seeing another woman and he wasn't brave enough to admit it.

She knew he was hiding something, but the thought of another woman had only been a fleeting one. He had been acting like a little boy with a secret that he wasn't going to tell no matter what she did to provoke him. Another woman, that was so hard for Lynn to believe, or was it?

"Lynn, I'll be late getting home tonight."

"How come?"

"I've got to go to Tom's house to help him put up some drywall."

"What's the telephone number?"

"What telephone number?"

"The telephone number for Tom."

"What do you need that for?"

"In case of an emergency."

"It's the new house. You know, the one they just bought. It doesn't have a phone yet because they haven't moved into it."

"Okay, then take the cell phone with you."

"I'll leave it in the car so I won't lose it. Most likely I won't hear it ring if you call."

"Sure, fine, whatever."

Lynn wasn't going to try to figure out why Sam wasn't coming home on time. He had too many excuses to cover all of the bases.

"Since you're going to be late, I'll go to Missy's house for a while. Make sure you get yourself some dinner. I don't plan to cook because I won't know what time to have it ready."

Sam shook his head in agreement.

The two of them exchanged no more words until they reached their destination.

"Sam, I love you," said Lynn as she pushed on the door of the pickup truck to climb out and hurry on to her place of employment at Mary's Bar and Grill. "Call me later, please?"

"If I have time," replied Sam as he tried to hurry her along so he could continue on his way to his job.

Before closing the pickup truck door, Lynn spotted something shiny wedged between the seat frame and the door frame. She reached to pick it up, but it wouldn't budge.

"Sam, there's something caught over here," she said pointing at the object. "If you get a chance, try to pry it out of there. It looks like a silver, hoop-style earring. Did your girlfriend who lost the lipstick also lose the earring? Have you got a secret life I don't know about?"

Lynn's question was not a poke of fun. She was serious, but she had to hide the meaning behind a fake smile.

Sam didn't smile.

"See you later, Honey. Remember, I love you," he whispered as she moved away from the pickup truck.

Lynn turned so Sam couldn't see her face and especially her eyes that were glistening with unshed tears.

There was no doubt about it, Sam was seeing another woman.

"Who could it be? What have I done to make him search elsewhere?" Lynn asked herself as she ran into the building.

Sam was stymied. He didn't know how to tell Lynn that those items she was finding in the truck belonged to her.

It happened about a month earlier. When Sam went to pick up Lynn at work she was over in the corner of the bar all by herself. She wasn't acting right.

"Lynn, are you ready to go home?" asked Sam as he carefully watched Lynn's reaction.

"No, I want a drink," she slurred as she swung her arms around herself like she was fighting someone off of her.

"Looks like you've had enough," returned Sam as he reached for Lynn's arm.

"I've only had one."

"Come on, Lynn. Let's go."

Lynn pulled herself up from the chair and let Sam lead her out of the bar to the pickup truck.

"Where'd you get those silver earrings?" Sam asked as he helped her into the truck.

"John gave them to me. You know John, the other bartender. He bought them for his girlfriend but they broke up. He isn't seeing her anymore so he didn't want to keep these as a reminder," she said as she waved her hand at the silver hoop.

"I thought John was married?"

"He is, but he also had a girlfriend."

"Where'd you get the red lipstick?"

"Same place. John didn't want it."

"Sure was nice of him," Sam said sarcastically. "Did John give you anything else?"

"What do you mean?" asked Lynn in a defensive tone.

"Just asking if he gave you anything else. Seems to be awfully generous, John does."

"He's just a nice guy."

"Your boss called me a little while ago. He said you were acting strange."

"I'm not acting strange at all," she continued to slur.

"He said you went totally bonkers on them and started throwing things. Do you remember that?"

"No, I didn't do that. I couldn't do that. I work there. I don't want to lose my job."

"Jack said you were throwing anything you could find at John."

"Nooooo–I'm sure I didn't. John's my friend, my close friend."

"How close, Lynn?"

"Huh? A friend. You know what a friend is, don't you?"

"Yeah, sure. Do you know what time it is?"

"Not exactly."

"Look at your watch."

Lynn dropped her unsteady head down to glance at her watch and tried to focus in on the small face. Her head seemed to be moving around uncontrollably as she looked and squinted and looked again at the small timepiece.

It was nine o'clock. She had gotten off work at five o'clock. Why was it so late?

"That can't be right," she slurred.

"Look around you, Lynn. It's dark outside. You didn't call me when you got off work. What happened?"

Lynn shook her head as she tried to focus. "I had a drink. That's all. I had a drink."

"Who served you that drink?"

"John did."

"Are you sure?"

"Sure, I remember him asking me what I wanted. He was all friendly and such."

"What do you mean by and such?"

"Well, you know, smiling at me, talking soft and sweet. Like you do sometimes when you're wanting me to go to bed."

"What happened next?"

"I don't remember. The last thing I recall was looking at the clock and seeing six thirty. I don't know why that time sticks in my mind, but I saw the big, giant clock with the arms, both of them, pointing at six thirty."

"Don't you remember anything else?"

"Well, I didn't go to bed with him if that's what you think."

"How do you know? You said you don't remember."

"I just know. Okay? A woman knows these things."

"Yeah, right. Try to remember anything else."

Lynn focused on what was flashing through her mind. Most of it didn't make sense. Just bright colors and a whirlwind of faces swirling around in front of her.

John was floating in front of her mind's eye. He was so handsome with his neatly cut, light brown beard that closely followed his jawline. His smile was so pleasant until her vision of it became a distorted clown's smile like someone laughing at her, not with her.

Then she saw John's hand. He poured the shot of rum in the shot glass.

That was fine. There wasn't anything wrong with that picture.

He grabbed her tall glass of Coke and dropped more ice into it, followed by some little, white objects.

Everything was floating through the air into the tall, glass of Coke. Plop, plop, plop went the ice cubes followed by the plink, plink, plink of what? Ice chips?

Lynn didn't think it was anything other than ice chips. After all, John was her friend.

He picked up the shot glass and poured the rum into the tall glass, mixing it with the Coke. He swirled the swizzle stick around a couple of times and then again as he held the giant glass of Coke up to the direction of the overly bright light before replacing the glass on the top of the bar in front of Lynn, who was busy talking to a friend.

John grabbed the money she had placed in front of her glass and rang up the sale on the cash register.

"Lynn, here's to good times. I love to share the fun with my friends," he said as he raised his glass to clink together with hers.

She took a sip of her drink and remembered no more except looking at the giant clock at six thirty.

John had given her something. John had put something in her glass.

That fleeting memory disappeared when Lynn passed out on the front seat of the pickup truck. Sam carried her into the house and placed her gently on the bed. He undressed her and covered her with a light blanket before he climbed onto the bed carefully and quietly beside her.

Lynn woke up the next morning feeling tired and groggy, but had no idea that she had been drugged.

"Sam, I'm so tired this morning," she said as she slapped cold water onto her face.

"You're working too hard, Honey."

Sam drove her to work with no words between them about what had happened the previous night.

John disappeared for a few weeks because his wife had him committed to a detoxification unit to get him off whatever he had shared with Lynn.

Lynn never knew what had happened, but somehow, somewhere she had lost four hours of her life. She didn't know her good friend and coworker, John, could have killed her with his actions.

All Lynn knew was that she wasn't going to drink anymore. In the past, she had always taken pride in the fact that she could drink a lot and still maintain control of her surroundings. Losing four hours of her life wasn't going to happen again, not if she had anything to do with it.

Her mind went back to a problem she could remember. The last thing she was thinking about before the missing four hours was that she was so worried about the lipstick and the earring she found in the pickup truck.

Lynn decided that as soon as she saw Sam she was going to ask him outright why he was seeing another woman.

Before the work day was over a delivery man stopped in the bar and deposited a bouquet of a dozen, long stemmed, red roses with a card that read:

LYNN
THE ONLY WOMAN I'VE EVER LOVED.
SAM

Lynn never thought about the earring and lipstick again.

Fishtrap Dam

George Justice

I knew the long drive to Sissy's house would be my last before the road was closed for good, before the water rose to cover it altogether. I went despite Sissy's admonitions, a white-knuckles grip on the steering wheel and the bitter dissolve of a Xanax under my tongue. It was six miles from the time I turned off the main highway to her house, six miles up a knurled desolate strip—four miles of crumbling blacktop and another two miles of what can only be described as a sled road—all the way to the head of Upper Pompey. The blacktop was always good for a copperhead or two when the sun was high; its warm asphalt, to hear Sissy tell it, was the perfect antidote for the cold blooded, builders of the dam included. The dam had taken nearly four years to complete; four years for Sissy and her neighbors—all six miles of them—to pack up and get out, but then Sissy had her own ideas about leaving. I'd spent thirty years going back and forth to Sissy's and knew exactly where the blacktop ended, it just up and ran out, its impermanence giving way to a soft, tire-worn dirt track—half of it washed out about half the time. It had little meaning except to the few who lived beyond it, little renown barring its meander along the river and what seemed set aside for lovers and those angling for catfish.

Most days crows and hawks circled overhead, gliding on warm updrafts—currents so familiar with Upper Pompey's long verdant valley—

and on the lookout for flesh, dead or alive. They were like wisps, shadowed silhouettes and silent as dreams, part of mother nature's finely scripted balance.

She lived there alone, Sissy did, in a white frame house too big for one; what she'd bought for next to nothing on account of the narratives that had grown up around it, mostly the ghosts that stalked it of a night. Restless souls according to locals—those crossed-over but who remained detached and unforgiven—looking for a place to rest. According to Sissy, it couldn't have been more ideal: those lost souls providing her company year round and the good fortune of being watched over while she slept.

Sissy never bothered to marry or entertain those so inclined. Other than a long-tailed Tom that never seemed to get much further than the deep, rounded cushions on the porch swing (even when there was a mouse for the taking), Sissy chose what she liked to call "the untarnished state of privacy"—separateness holding her to a greater concord, out and away from the stock and natter of life. But then, too, there were the few chickens she kept, Road Island Reds mostly, that clucked and scratched about and warned of snakes, and who faithfully came whenever she called, pecking in agitated motions at the corn middling she scattered like someone throwing rice at a wedding.

From the corner of my eye, a leghorn rooster, a likely runaway and in a still-life pose by the side of the road—barely visible in the cover of weeds and with a June bug in its beak—brought me back to the truth and tremor of the day, my goodbye as correctness would have it. I thought more than once to turn around, to let Sissy's memory alone sustain me, but then there was something—as always—that held me to a more solemn course, to a deeper resolve, though I could never be sure what it might be, only that it kept me windward for the most part and clinging to good intention. And though I tried to focus only on the road ahead, scattered pieces of life so expressive of Sissy's infernal solace came full view—mud yards and their borders of weeds, forgotten washtubs on smokehouse walls, dilapidated porch steps and endless want-me-nots in between the scandal of crocks chipped and cracked and holding on for the sake of holding on. And those endless fencerows that no longer served a purpose, busted and rusted and tangled, and helping to blight the near-perfect splendor of Kentucky's Eastern Appalachia.

From one patch of ground to the next barns and houses, faded and brittle and given to last gasps, sat hollow-eyed and yawning, bearing only the chink and tide of remembering; blanched of the last vestiges of color and left to the joining of grays and browns and rot.

And, too, there were the mailboxes, splintered and aging sentinels, eaten up in cattails and briars and climbers lost to any name but hell vine; empty and silent, listing and waiting to bear the freshness of news, but ultimately settling like good servants for the web of spiders, rust, and rain.

I slipped the Jeep into low gear when the blacktop ran out, then stopped by the river's shallows—anything to delay my coming, the static rush of its waters adding its own hint of melancholy, a temper not altogether unfamiliar given Sissy's detraction, what she now aspired to disavow.

Magpies squawked at me from nearby willows, their heads careening this way and that, on the lookout for morsels slow and unsuspecting, unmatched for the stealth of avengers yet indignant of being brought to an end. I imagined Sissy being the same—indignant to those who would bring her to an end, her footing more and more like softening firmament, much like the silt beneath the rocks in the river. There was a discursiveness to fast, running water, its dash between the rocks and the froth it stirred; a fleetingness to its cascade, hurrying like the rattle of wind through cottonwoods. It held me captive, weighed me with its spell, somehow reminding me why I'd come and why I needed to defer to Sissy's decision, her final resolution.

I stayed by the river until my courage returned, the way I when uncertainty had the upper hand. Except for the jostling of the Jeep and the hum of its engine, I'd never felt so alone. The thoughts of Sissy and our times together—the short span we were allotted to this physical realm—were stark reminders of how fleeting our paths had been. It was times like these that I couldn't help but think of life as a yardstick and how I was down to my last couple inches.

For the next two miles the richest and deepest evergreens darkened the forest floor and dampened the scurrying of ground squirrels, oblivious but to their own back and forth. The last mile—the steepest—gave way to treeless meadows as barren as burlap, and a long stretch of gravel reaching right up to Sissy's front porch where she sat rocking and watching the trail of dust rolling up behind my Jeep.

Sissy was the last of the holdouts. She'd stood her ground, right out there in the middle of her yard, right there next to her snowball bush and the half cord of hardwood she'd spilt, right there in the face of lawyers and them with hard hats, and her with an axe in her hand.

I was there the day they came, midafternoon and just as I was taking a pone of bread off the stove. I'd seen them all before, faces puffed with spite and spit and grainy as a cellar door. Only this time dragging poor ol' Sheriff Vaught Breathit along to serve the notice to quit, his face as long and sorrowful as the redbone hound he kept as a constant companion in the back of his pickup.

The dam was a foregone conclusion, passed and litigated by those who would never have to know its affects firsthand. Nothing left now but to clear out, evict and remove what remained of life, love, and memories; all those who once worked and played, fought and prayed side by side; all that went into fomenting the valley's grassy slopes into an amalgamation of families and friends—even foes—and now with hardly a thought except to recount what once was.

"One week!" they said to Sissy. "One week 'fore the 'lectric's cut." There was little she could expect after that, they told her, except the inescapable onslaught of rising water and darkness.

They left immediately afterwards...all except for Sheriff Breathit. He didn't stay long or say much, just that he was sorry...about a lot of things...particularly about what had passed between him and Sissy over the years, about how he was never quite able to find the right key, though he tried for the better part of twenty years, to unlock that invisible door that separated them...and about wishing he could have been more—the one she pined for. And how he knew about her ongoing "botherments" as he called them—botherments for which she steadfastly refused treatment. I turned to walk away, but he caught me by the arm and said I should stay, that maybe it was good that I heard what he had to say, what he'd carried inside him for so long.

I stood there waiting, but it was like a valve had suddenly been shut off, like there was too much to say and the time long passed for it to do any good. Still we stood there in the light of awkwardness, his considerable deep breaths and the over-and-again pawing at the back of his neck; his helping himself to the sadness on Sissy's face and moving gravel about with the toe of his boot. Finally, he pinched the bridge of his nose and said how deeply grieved he was that it had come to this, and if it was left up to him, nobody would ever be forced off their land, that everyone of God's children would have the right to choose where they'd spend the last of their days. We thanked him without saying, our language silent but no less real.

"I won't be back," he told Sissy. "Our time—yours and mine—has come and gone, best I can tell." He gave her a long look and a tight-lip, something akin to a smile, before turning to leave. He made it all the way to his truck before turning around. He took several deep breaths then raised his hand in a simple goodbye. He rolled away, slow and not enough to raise even the slightest dust. We watched after him till he disappeared down the hill, then went to sit on the porch; iced tea, cornbread and butter the only things that seemed worth our efforts, even then they were heavy and without the slightest savor.

The rest of the day was much like I expected it to be—without substance. We were long past the point of talking. I already knew what she planned to do. She'd told me often enough. I had no reason to doubt her, and I sure as hell had enough sense not to try and talk her out of it.

"Take what you want," she said, but I took nothing, not even the family album. I had no one to leave it to, and other than me, neither did she. Who would have cared one way or the other? She did, however, convince me to take the cat.

I wasn't there when she did it—when she and her sliver-plated derringer said "No" to the tumor metastasizing next to her temporal lobe... right about the time her house became her pyre. To this day, I choose to believe it was glorious—she and her house giving way to a new day; a goodbye as earnest as it was peace giving, as loving to herself as it was to anyone who knew her. Private and sacred. As gossamer as angel wings and as blighted as her valley—quiet and still under an inland sea.

The Highway Woman

Rebecca Williams Spindler

"MAMA! We're outta peanut butter!"

Blowing into the kitchen like a gusty gulf stream comes Emma Jane (EJ) Riley, 28, dressed in her Waffle House uniform. She pulls her daughter, Avery, 12, aside and peeks into the plastic jar.

"Aw, there's plenty in there to finish your sandwich...and your brother's."

Sleepy headed, Eliason, 9, wonders in rubbing at his eyes. "Peanut butter, again?" He whines.

"We're keeping those Georgia peanut farmers in business," EJ replies with a kiss to his cheek. Both of EJ's children are bean poles just like her. Scrawny yet with iron bones that can withstand a few good licks. Avery, with her freckled cheeks and auburn hair, is a spitting image of her mother. Discouraged, Avery pokes a knife and digs what bit she can to spread across a couple slices of bread.

The back screen door slams as Mamaw Riley bustles in, pocket book at the crook in her arm. "My washer's on the fritz, repairman can't come out until next Thursday."

EJ stops dead in her tracks. All eyes in the room fall on the heaping laundry basket by the back door.

"Avery, after school you'll need to hand wash the underwear and socks in the sink." EJ ignores the billboards of disgust on her daughter's and son's faces. "And Eli, you'll need to hang everything up in the shower. Let's hope it's all dry by morning."

The children's shoulders slump as they pack their lunches into their backpacks. EJ ushers them out the door and watches as they woefully climb into her mother's Buick. Mamaw gives a "bye" tap to the horn as they make their way down the long, grass driveway.

Potter's Hollow is dewy and green on this March morning. Flecks of yellow daffodils dot the valley. The mist is rising and EJ takes in a long, cool breath. She snags her sweater off a hook and her travel mug of coffee. Her glitzy Las Vegas key chain rattles as she locks up the house. The door to the '97 Ford pick-up creaks as she climbs inside. She pumps the gas pedal a couple times and turns the engine. There's a smoky sputter, then the truck comes alive. She can't seem to part with her daddy's F-150. It's a rusty relic, but a trusty one at that!

EJ navigates the narrow roads through the holler like a pro, steers with one finger mostly while she swigs coffee with her other hand. Then she flicks on 97.5 WAMZ as Garth Brooks croons into the truck cab. Her blue eyes glisten as she taps a photo of her dear departed Dad taped to her sun visor.

As she works the clutch and shifts the 4-on-the-floor with the grace of a ballerina, the windy road leads to the highway. Then EJ notes the gas gage. The orange needle on E brings her a deep sense of dread. She digs in her wallet and finds only a few crumpled dollars. Then she checks her watch.

"Get me to work, Daddy, I'll take it from there," she pleads as she touches his photo.

The pick-up practically coasts into the Waffle House parking lot. EJ hops out, checks her hair and face in the side mirror and, appeased with her appearance, she enters the establishment.

The regular crew of Cory at the grill, Ladelle at the register, and Ashiqua serving tables, are busy about their business. The clanking of plates, the sizzle of pork, and smell of burnt coffee fills the tiny diner. EJ fastens her apron and eagerly joins the morning meal circus.

Two gentlemen, one dressed in a suit and tie, taps at his empty coffee mug. She brings a smile and obliges with a refill. The other man in a flannel shirt and trucker cap meets her eyes and gives his order.

"Waffles with a side of bacon."

"Yes sir," she replies. "And for you?"

The suited man adds, "Country ham and eggs, scrambled. And keep the coffee coming."

EJ gives a cordial nod and reports the order back to Cory. Then she helps Ashiqua brew up more coffee.

"Bet you're counting the days until graduation," EJ says.

"I sure am! Got my C.N.A. license so I'll be working at a clinic this summer then off to Berea College in the fall."

"Good for you, girl," adds Ladelle. She places a wash-worn, fifty-year-old hand to Ashiqua's youthful, manicured one.

During this exchange between her co-workers, EJ gets a knot in her throat. Her teen years are a blur to her now, she can barely recall her high school graduation. Maybe because she didn't cross that stage with her cap and gowned classmates. Her G.E.D. ceremony happened on a week night, where she had baby Avery squawking on her hip as she grabbed her certificate and quickly fled to girl's bathroom. Clutching Avery, EJ sank down in a stall and wept along with her toddler.

DING! A bell above the door announces a senior couple who enters the diner. Ashiqua greets them and shows them to a table. EJ wipes down a vacated table near the two men.

"We are in a dire situation," says the suited man. "Recruiting truckers is like finding needles in a hay stack!"

"You're singing to the choir," says the other man. "My drivers can't pull any more runs than we're already doing. You're gonna need to step up your game at the trucking school."

"I know," quietly answers the suited man. "I'm about to make a big announcement at the trucking conference today."

"Is it the deal we talked about?" inquires the man in the trucker cap.

"The very one," replies the suited man, loosening his tie. "Waiving the entry fee into my truck driving school and giving a two-thousand dollar bonus for completion."

"And 100% guaranteed job placement for certified drivers with companies like mine," adds the other man.

EJ's ears perk.

"Clucks and cakes!" barks Cory from the grill. EJ swoops by, picks up the food plates, and delivers them to the men's table where she's met with nods and curled lips. Without missing a beat, she also tops off their coffees.

"'Scuse me, sir," EJ mutters. "I heard you say you run a trucking school?"

"That's right, missy," says the suited man between forked bites of eggs. "Why? You gotta fella who's interested?"

EJ's spine straightens as a rolling boil rises in her belly. She uses every fiber of her being to fix her feminine and determined face.

"Yes, sir...I mean, no, sir. Me. I'm the one who's interested." She flashes a proud, toothy grin.

The suited man keeps his eyes on his plate, gorging on forkful after forkful of eggs and ham. The other man in the cap bathes his stack of waffles in syrup. Neither of these men gives her a second glance.

"Can I get ya anything else?"

The suited man only grunts as he slurps his coffee and the other man shakes his head, "no." She pulls their check from her apron pocket and places it on the table. As she's ready to spin away, EJ hesitates. She just has to take a chance. She leans over the shoulder of the man in the trucker cap.

"See that Ford outside," she says pointing to her daddy's pick-up. "I've done every oil change myself, rotated tires, spark plugs, and me and my cousin changed the exhaust on it last month. Taught myself how to replace the clutch cable too," she quips with a slight giggle. "You can learn anything on YouTube these days."

The men's jaws drop as they rubber neck from the old Ford to EJ. "Hmpf. A wildflower like you did all that?" questions the suited man.

"I never went out for sports as a kid. Guess my hobby was being a grease monkey like my Dad."

"Got a clean driving record?" asks the man in the trucker cap.

"Yes, sir. I sure do! Never had a ticket in my life."

The suited man reads her name tag. "EJ? You got a real name, girl?"

"Emma Jane Riley, sir."

The suited man looks to the man in the trucker cap and they nod in unison. Then the suited man reaches into his breast pocket and presents a business card to EJ.

"Well, Miss Riley, my name is Elroy Simmons. I look forward to receiving your application to my truck driving school."

The man in the trucker hat chimes in, "I'm Chuck Connors, owner of Connors Logistics. Pass that driving test and you look me up."

EJ beams. She steadies her arm as not to spill the pot of coffee. With her free hand, she accepts his card. "YES, SIR!" She tucks the business card securely into her apron pocket. "Thank you, Mr. Simmons and Mr. Connors," she says brightly.

EJ returns behind the counter and parks the coffee pot on the warmer. Her hand slides down into the apron pocket and pats the business card. Ladelle leans over to her. EJ's rosy cheeks and wide grin are unavoidable.

"You look like you just won the lottery, dear," Ladelle says.

"Oh Ladelle, I think I did."

"You've been showing up here every week for the past nine years. About time you make something happen. Get on outta here, and don't look back." Ladelle gives her an encouraging nudge.

Later that afternoon, EJ stands at a gas pump and pulls twelve dollars of tip money from her uniform. After filling the pick-up, she journeys her way back home with Mr. Simmons's business card in full view on her dashboard.

While Avery and Eli half-heartedly handwash the family's undergarments in the kitchen sink, EJ pecks on a tablet on loan from Avery's school. At the stove, Mamaw is cooking up a skillet of Hamburger Helper.

"Driving a big rig? I don't know, EJ," Mamaw says worriedly.

"On Mr. Connors' website it said he needs drivers for his mid-size trucks. That's a lot easier than backing up a semi. Not that I couldn't handle a semi. Once I pass that CDL test, I can be a commercial driver for anybody or even be employed all on my own!"

"You'd be gone for days at time," Mamaw continues.

"Would you really, Mama?" Eliason's voice innocently quivers.

"Not necessarily," replies EJ. She gives her son a reassuring smile. "Connors needs drivers for the triangle. Louisville to Cincinnati to

Indianapolis and back to Louisville. It's a day job and I'd be back in time for supper."

"Lucky you, Mama! I can't wait until I get my driver's license." Excitement rings in Avery's voice.

"All in good time, Baby Girl. With a trucking job I'll be making more in one year than I would in three years at the Waffle House. I could show you all Kentucky, Ohio, and Indiana."

With that, Eliason starts singing "IN-DEE-ANNA, IN-DEE-ANNA!" which cracks up Mamaw and her cackling makes the whole group whoop like cranes. Having the kitchen fill with warm laughter is something EJ's not experienced in a long while.

"Plus, I could afford us a real vacation. Maybe even to Florida!"

"Not without me, you don't!" bellows Mamaw.

EJ gives her mother a playful wave. "Okay, fine. You can be our 4th wheel in Florida, Mamaw. Gonna use my first check to get you a new washing machine."

"I never pictured my daughter as a truck-driving woman," Mamaw declares.

"Why not? Hey! This girl's dream is 'bout to come true!"

The group huddles around EJ as she gazes lovingly into each one of their sweet faces. Then, she turns to the tablet screen, her eyes grow wide and her expression is confident as she hits the submit button on her truck driving school application.

No Shades of Gray

Linda Hudson Hoagland

"You have cancer, Ellen. You should start getting your affairs in order to make it easier on yourself and your loved ones," said the doctor as his face took on the humbled appearance of one who could do no more to help her.

At the age of fifty five, Ellen was thinking about all of things she had accomplished in her lifetime. To some people fifty five is not physically old, but to Ellen, her age was something that was mental. Ellen's mind felt old because she had had to learn so very much, and then go on living with herself and with those around her who were prone to rushing to judgment.

There were occurrences in Ellen's life that she discussed with no one. She knew she would be judged and maybe she should be, but she also knew they would not accept her explanation, not here in the Bible belt where there are no shades of gray.

Ellen's days were coming to an end because she had discovered she had cancer just, as she predicted she would after her father succumbed to the dreaded disease.

She didn't want to die without those around her knowing that her life wasn't the easy, run of the mill life that they expected for her to have lived.

She had lived.

She had endured.

She had survived.

She lay in her bed thinking about what her living had given her and cost her.

The very first time she had ever had sex produced her beautiful baby boy named Eddy. It also produced a divorce after the birth of her second son, Aaron.

She had endured a bad marriage, a long eight years of single motherhood that was followed by another marriage that lasted for only six months. The second time she should have known better, but the truth was that she was lonely.

Mike was a nice man and he had two daughters the same ages as her two sons. It was only a matter of days for Ellen to discover that the oil of Mike's two daughters and the water of her two sons didn't mix well at all.

She preferred the loneliness to constant fighting, so she put an end to the second marriage quickly.

She survived a lost love, lost friends, and lost self-esteem, and then she met and married her third husband, the one who had been with her for over twenty-five years and would be by her side when her eyes closed for the last time.

"Sonny, you've met Ed, the father of my sons. What did you think about him?" Ellen asked her husband.

"I think he is a sorry man. He lost you, and when he was around you I could tell that he was really sorry that he caused the loss to happen. He did, didn't he? He was the one who caused the divorce?"

"Yes, except truthfully it wasn't for the reasons that were explained to people. I didn't want the truth to get out."

"What was the truth? The real truth?"

"I didn't love him was what I told everybody when I was asked. The fact that he was using my oldest son for a football to kick and abuse was the real reason. It was one of several."

"What else was there?" Sonny asked.

"He drank every day, hard liquor, when he was at lunch and then again after work. He was chasing other women including my best friend, Annie. I just couldn't handle it anymore. We didn't have money for food, rent, or anything because he spent it all on booze and camera equipment for his so-called hobby of photography."

"Well, don't think about him and what was wrong with your marriage, think about the two beautiful sons that were created as the result of your union."

"Thanks, Sonny, I just wanted you to know the truth about Ed, the father of our sons, yours and mine. They have always been your sons, not Ed's, even though their birth certificates declare differently. They learned to love you when Eddy was just entering the teen years and Aaron was two years behind him. After they lost their grandfather to cancer, who had spent eight years being their father figure, you filled that enormous hole in their lives for them and they will never forget it, neither will I."

"I love them, too."

Ellen dozed off to sleep for a few moments and then awoke with a start. The medicine she was given to control her pain was actually controlling her life, what there was left of it.

"Sonny, did I ever tell you about Jack?" she whispered to her husband as he held her hand.

"Not much, you never really got into how you felt about him, but I knew you loved him. I never knew what happened or why he isn't here sitting next to you."

"Jack was my life between my first husband, Ed, and my second husband, Mike," she said in a voice that seemed to be growing weaker with the breath expended for each word she uttered.

"Maybe you shouldn't talk now, Ellen."

"I want to talk. I need to talk. I need to tell you about Jack and why he isn't here sitting next to me. I need to tell you how happy I am that you are here and are the reason I have lived and loved and survived."

"All right, but stop whenever you need to."

"I was going through the divorce from Ed when I met Jack. I can look back now and laugh at myself because I can see the truth oozing out of his pores, but I couldn't see it then through my love struck eyes."

Ellen paused and closed her eyes as she remembered. A hint of a smile caused her mouth to turn up slightly at each end.

* * *

"Bertha, those guys keep watching us," I said as I pointed to two men sitting across the room.

"Yeah, I know. I like the blonde."

"So do I. He's a real gorgeous man," I said dreamily as I sipped on my rum and Coke.

I decided to go play some tunes on the jukebox. I grabbed a couple of quarters and walked across the room where I would be closer to the watchers. As I studied the list of music selections I listened to their conversation.

"I like the blonde."

"She's fat. I like the little dark-haired girl."

I felt myself bristling with that remark, but it was true. I was a fat size sixteen but it was a great improvement over the size twenty that I had been.

"She's not fat. She's just the right size. I like my women healthy. At least she doesn't have a mustache."

I laughed out loud. I didn't want to do that but I did. I punched a few buttons on the jukebox and walked across the room trying to straighten up so I wouldn't have to tell Bertha what I was laughing about. I didn't think she would find it very funny.

A couple of drinks later, the two men joined us at our table.

"I'm Jack," he said with a happy slur, "and this handsome man is Wayne. We haven't seen you two around here before."

"We've been here a couple of times but it's usually later in the evening," I said in explanation.

"I'm glad you're here earlier or that we stayed later. Whichever way it is, I'm glad."

"So am I," I said with an obvious sigh.

Jack buttonholed me conversation wise, and Bertha was getting angrier by the moment.

"Ellen, I'm married but my wife and I are separated. Are you tied to anyone?"

"I'm going through a divorce right now. It should be final soon, I hope. But I do have two small sons."

"I have kids, too. I have six kids so you know where my obligations are first."

"I wouldn't have it any other way."

I could see angry steam rising from Bertha's head so I decided to go to the ladies room so I could discover what her problem was.

"What's the matter? Don't you like Wayne?" I asked with obvious annoyance.

"No, as a matter of fact, I don't. You know I liked the looks of Jack."

"That's too bad, Bertha, because he liked the looks of me. I can't help that, you know," I said with my voice dripping with sarcasm.

"I want to leave."

"Now?"

"Yes."

"I'll tell Jack and meet you at the car."

I was almost in tears because I truly didn't want to leave. I was so very much attracted to Jack. It was so unexpected for me to react that way to any man, especially since I was going through a truly ugly divorce from Ed.

"Jack, Bertha is in a snit. She wants to leave and I have to leave with her."

"Okay, then. Maybe we'll run into you again."

Out the door I went. He didn't ask me for my telephone number nor did he indicate that he wanted to spend any more time with me. I was crying by the time I reached the car.

Jack never left my mind.

I met Jack before my divorce from Ed was final and I wanted nothing to interfere with that final decree.

* * *

"Ellen, you don't have to talk anymore," said Sonny as he soothed his dying wife.

"Yes, I do. I have to tell you what I've never told anyone else. I can't go to my grave being the only one who ever knew the truth about the woman you are sitting next to."

Ellen closed her eyes for a few moments.

Sonny thought she was drifting off to sleep but she started talking again.

* * *

"Oh, God, I'm pregnant," I cried as I ran to the bathroom to throw up.

I didn't want to be pregnant. I wanted out of a marriage that was going to end with a blood bath eventually if it were allowed to continue. I couldn't take Ed's drinking and screwing around anymore. That's what I told myself.

The truth was that I wanted Jack.

"Ed, do you remember when you moved back in here and decided to prove your manhood? Do you remember when you did that?" The tone of my voice hinted at the fact that I wasn't a happy camper.

"What are you talking about, Ellen?"

"That time you decided to make another attempt at being husband and wife and you moved back in here, don't you remember?" I said sarcastically.

"Of course, I remember. What about it?"

"I'm pregnant, Ed. That's what about it."

"Are you sure?"

"I'm throwing up every morning."

"What are you going to do?"

"What am I going to go? This is not my problem alone! You had a hand in it so to speak."

"Okay what are we going to do? Do you want me to move back in and forget about the divorce?" he said with a sound of hope present.

"No, that's the last thing I want."

"You were pregnant when we got married. Eddy is proof of that."

"I don't want any more living proof of my stupidity. When I got pregnant with Eddy it was my very first time of ever having sex, and you know that. Aaron was planned, you know that, too. I didn't want Eddy to be an only child. I wanted both of my sons and I wouldn't give them up for anyone or anything."

"Then you're going to keep this new kid?"

"No, I want an abortion. I don't want any more reasons for the marriage to go on forever and ever."

"Are you sure?"

"Yes, I want an abortion and you've got to help me pay for it." I said it out loud. The thought that had been forming in my mind was put into words.

"I'll have to borrow some money. How much do you need?"

"Three hundred dollars would be about half of it."

"You've already checked into haven't you?"

"I don't want this baby, Ed. Don't be telling anybody about this. I don't want anyone to know, not your mother, not the judge, not your lawyer, nobody, do you understand me?"

"I'll get the money."

As determined as I was with Ed about wanting the abortion, I was really scared about the whole thing. I knew I couldn't afford another baby to care for because I had to work, which meant I had to pay a babysitter. I wanted to take care of the two sons I already had and another baby was going to be a giant obstacle that I was afraid I wouldn't be able to overcome. I'm not really as hard hearted as I sounded but, God help me, I didn't feel I had any choice.

The procedure was performed and I was no longer pregnant.

I knew God wasn't happy.

I knew Ed wasn't happy.

I knew I wasn't happy.

But it was done.

About a month later Bertha persuaded me to go out into the world again.

I found Jack.

My divorce had become final and I was no longer tied to Ed in any way except that he was the father of my two sons. I would meet Jack every day after work in a local bar until the fateful St. Patrick's Day when we made love until the wee hours of the morning.

"Oh, God, I'm pregnant," was my cry a few weeks later, except this time I was happy about it.

* * *

"Ellen, you need to get some sleep. You've been talking too long," said Sonny as he tried to stop Ellen's confessions to the secrets he wasn't sure he wanted to know.

"I have to tell you, Sonny. You have to know what kind of person I am, or was. I'm not like that now. I'm just a plain vanilla, ordinary type of woman except that I have a past. It's a past that no one knows about except me. I'm sure the men in my former life have forgotten about the heartache and grief I had to endure. I want you to know why I am the way I am," she said in a pleading tone as her voice started to fade.

Sonny nodded his head so she would not get upset. He would sit and listen to whatever she had to say, even if he didn't want to hear it.

* * *

Oh God, I wanted that baby, my love child, the proof of my love for Jack and the proof of his love for me. Morning sickness was becoming more and more evident each day. I was becoming pale and sickly looking, and I had no energy.

"Ellen, are you all right?" asked Jack when he entered the bar to meet me. We never met anywhere else, it was always at the bar.

"Sure, just a little tired. Can you come by the house tonight? I need to talk to you without a crowd around us."

"No, I've got to get home. Make sure the kids are okay."

"I thought your wife had the kids?"

"She does. I'm living at home."

"Why didn't you tell me?"

"We can't talk about that now."

"When can we talk about it? I have something I have to tell you, Jack. When can I do that?" I said as I choked back the tears.

"Later, Ellen," he said as he walked away from me and out the door to his car so that he could drive home to his wife and six children.

It was later, all right. He showed up at my door two weeks after I discovered I was the other woman. He was drunk, of course.

"Ellen, I love you, Ellen," he slurred as he hung all over me at my front door.

"Not enough, Jack," I said as I struggled to keep him upright.

"Let's go to bed, Ellen. I need you, Ellen."

"No, Jack. We need to talk."

"Don't want to talk. Want to make love. Want to love you until..."

"Until what? Until you've shot your wad, that's it, isn't it, Jack? Wifey not giving you any?" I said in a mocking tone.

Jack blinked himself into a semi sober frame of mind. "What's the matter with you?" he slurred at me.

"I'm pregnant, Jack."

"What do you want me to do about it?"

"I'm going to have this baby, Jack. You're going to have another little mouth to feed," I said in a taunt.

"That's why my wife and I separated. She was pregnant and I didn't want another mouth to feed. I told her if she didn't get rid of the baby, I would be gone," he said without any hesitation or slurring.

"Is that what you're telling me? I have no choice? I have to get an abortion?"

"It is if you want me around."

"You've gone back to your wife, isn't she handling your manly duties?"

"I don't love her, Ellen. I love you. I don't want any more children. I will divorce my wife and marry you but not if you're pregnant. Do you understand?"

"Yes," I said as I led him to my bedroom and my bed.

I loved him. What else could I do but get an abortion? The procedure was performed for the second time in my life. Jack contributed half of the cost. I cried for the loss of my first baby and I cried for the loss of my second baby.

God had gotten even with me. He knew I didn't want the first baby. He also knew how desperately I wanted the second baby.

Jack never returned to my bed.

* * *

"I wanted you to know about what I had done, Sonny. I wanted you to know that my life has been a struggle, but I survived. I wanted you to know the truth just in case someone else had a different version. I know that people around here in this small town of righteous individuals would not understand nor would they want to understand why I did what I did two different times. I want to know that you forgive me for what I've done because He already has. I want to go to the great beyond knowing that I haven't lived in vain."

"Ellen, I love you. Of course, I forgive you. That was part of your life where I wasn't included. I forgive anything that has happened before me and I forgive anything that has happened since me."

And with that, Ellen closed her eyes for the last time.

The Tomato Graveyard

Draco Sage

Jordan's cheeks were turning pink already from the sun, her wide brim hat tossed aside on a small mound of dirt. She wiped the sweat from her forehead with the back of her arm and huffed, all the while glaring at the wilting plants before her.

Stupid garden.

She heard the muffled tune of her ringtone from somewhere in the grass. On her hands and knees she felt for the phone around her and answered without glancing at the caller ID.

"Hello?"

"Uh-oh, what's wrong pumpkin?"

"Oh, hi Daddy." Jordan felt her anger start to deflate. She flopped on her back in the yard and began to twiddle a blade of grass between her fingers. Her father remained silent. He was still waiting for her to answer his question. She supposed she had come off a bit harsh in her greeting.

She sighed, "I'm giving up on gardening. I'm not cut out for this dig in the dirt, disturb the worms, murder all the tomatoes crap."

Jordan's father was chuckling before she even finished her sentence, his voice deep and rumbling like thunder. She rolled her eyes, but the malice in her expression was long gone. Her father had an uncanny ability to make even the biggest disasters seem flippant. Not that her inability to grow a plant that lasted more than a day or so was a disaster, just pathetic.

"Now, now, I don't think the tomatoes hold it against you, Jo."

"You haven't asked them. They're planning a coup—what's left of them anyways."

She could hear the grin in his voice when her father responded, "Well, I'll have to give them a talkin' to."

Jordan shot up out of the grass. "What?"

"I'm on my way, be there in about five minutes."

She scrambled to her feet and scooped up her hat. "Dad that's really not necessary, there's nothing you can do! They're all goners, just like my gardening ability. You don't have to go out of your way."

As she spoke she was stooped over with her trowel, prodding her dwindling plants and plucking up the deceased bodies of the ones that didn't make it. She was mortified that her father might see her garden, *perhaps I should call it a graveyard instead*, in such a state. She heard a truck turn onto her street.

"It's not out of my way, I came out to see you! I'd say that makes it exactly my way."

Jordan had her phone clenched between her ear and shoulder, listening to her father talk his nonsensical jokes as he drove and poked fun at her panic. He never did find it necessary that she straighten up for him, never cared if the house was in disarray or if she looked like she'd been rolling around in the dirt.

She glanced down to find that she, indeed, was covered in earth, because she *had* basically been rolling through the dirt just moments ago. She tossed the dead plants behind a nearby tree and spun on her heels to hurry inside for another shirt, but it was too late. Her father's truck was just pulling up in front of her house. She began frantically brushing dirt off her front with one hand, raising the other to waive as her father stepped out onto the lawn. She forgot all about her phone and it tumbled to the ground just as their call ended.

"Crap," she muttered to herself. She bent to gather her phone and looked back up to see her father striding toward her, a look of amusement painted across his high cheekbones. Jordan met him halfway between the front yard and the back, but as he reached out to hug her she held her hands up.

"Dad I'm an absolute mess," she protested.

Her father rolled his eyes, but respected her boundary. Instead, he tucked a wild hair behind her ear and said, "Don't fuss, Jo."

She offered him a half grin and a shrug, squinting up at him in the sun. His presence never ceased to appease her, even if she'd just been running around like a chicken with her head cutoff and wishing he'd give her more advance notice. Already the tendrils of calm were wrapping around her body.

"Your face is gettin' burnt, Jo. You oughta put some sunscreen on. I got some in the truck."

Jordan grabbed his wrist before he could rush back to his vehicle where he kept way more supplies than he actually needed, all for moments like this when his helicopter parent skills were on high alert.

"I'm alright, Daddy," she drawled. "I've got sunscreen inside. Come on, let's check out the cemetery...oh, I mean garden."

Her father laughed and Jordan swelled with pride. She was always excited to prove she was as quick witted as he and her mother had raised her to be.

Arm in arm they made their way to Jordan's sad, little garden. She chewed her lip as they arrived and her father squatted, baseball cap in his hands, and tsked over the sight that lay before him. *Ugh, he's going to disown me and revoke my farmer's daughter card.* She knew she was being dramatic, but considering her upbringing she really felt ashamed.

"Well, I won't say it looks good. But it's probably salvageable."

Jordan was shocked. "What? How?"

"Well for starters they're not getting enough water."

"I thought you said tomatoes loved the sun!"

"They do, Jo," her father smirked, "but they're not a desert plant."

Jordan crossed her arms, snubbing her nose at the shriveling crops by her feet. "Well, I do water them occasionally."

"Just enough to torture them, got it."

"Dad!"

Jordan's father got to his feet and held up his hands in defense. "Kidding, kidding. Anyways it's not entirely your fault. Looks like you've got a critter accomplice." He winked at her and held out a fallen leaf he'd picked from the dirt. There was a very clear chomp off the tip.

"Ugh, even the wildlife are against me," Jordan joked. "So now what?"

"I've got a couple ideas, let me run to the truck and get a few things." He dropped the chewed leaf in her hand, replaced his cap on his head, and strode off back toward the front.

"It's not sunscreen is it?" she hollered after him.

"That too!"

She shook her head. *Silly man.* Jordan tucked her sunhat under her arm briefly and began pulling her brunette hair back into a bun as she watched him rifle through the cabin. She recalled a time not too long ago when seeing her parents was a several hour venture. It had almost stayed that way, too. But, as luck would have it during one of Jordan's visits home, a longtime family friend listed their grandparents' house for sale. Jordan was signing paperwork before her vacation time was fully spent. Suddenly she never had to experience another heartache filled drive back to a city that was too busy and too full.

She smiled as the memory of telling her parents she was staying permanently swam into her mind's eye. Her mother had cried, and then promptly starting baking a celebratory cake. Her father had called everyone in their family, and all his friends too. Her parents gathered a huge group for a cookout, and her father made every burger well done no matter what the guests had asked for.

The slam of the tailgate drew her focus away from her thoughts and back to the present. She now saw that her father had pulled several railroad ties out of his truck bed and was carrying one in each arm down to the garden. Jordan jogged toward the vehicle so she could help out.

"Hey Jo," her father called as she passed him, "grab those other two railroad ties."

There were two more pieces of wood propped against the side of the truck. She peeked inside the bed to discover two large rolls of chicken fencing, a shovel, a bunch of cinderblocks, a hammer and nails, and several two by fours. With all the supplies strewn across the bed, Jordan was almost afraid to ask what on earth he had in the tool box stretched across the width of the truck.

She realized he'd come a little too prepared for her only having just told him about her gardening woes. *Oh for Pete's sake.*

Jordan grabbed the other railroad ties she'd been instructed to carry and followed her father's path to the backyard.

"Mom told you," she accused as she arrived where her father was already walking out measurements. She laid her wood alongside the others and arched an eyebrow at him. He grinned sheepishly, but didn't look at her.

"I told her not to tell you!" Jordan let her head droop back on her shoulders as she complained. She'd spoken to her mother just two days prior about her pitiful little garden, but she'd pleaded against her mother's insistence to let her father help. She hadn't wanted to bother him, nor had she wanted him to think that all his teaching on the farm growing up had been for naught.

"She's just lookin' out for you Jo Jo, don't be too hard on her now. You know how she takes such pride in her meddling. Now that hat don't do much good if you're staring directly into the sun. Here."

Jordan looked down just in time to catch the travel sized sunscreen he'd pulled from his pocket and hurled in her direction. She tried not to sulk too much as she applied it to her face. He was right, her mother did love to interfere, even if she had the best intentions. Jordan sighed. *Well it's too late to do anything about it now.*

"All right. What else do you want from the truck?"

"That's the spirit!" He looked up at her at last with a huge smile that made his crows' feet dance. It was infectious. "You got a wheelbarrow in the garage, right? Grab all 'em cinderblocks and the shovel. This isn't a permanent fence I'm setting up, mind you, but we can at least keep the critters out until I can build you somethin' prettier."

"Dad you don't have to–"

"Don't fuss now, you didn't move home to spend less time with us, ya know?"

She nodded. He was right again. She left him to his informal measuring system and by the time she returned with the wheelbarrow, cinderblocks, and shovel, he was already making a hole in the dirt with her forgotten trowel.

"This might work better, mister impatient." She handed him the shovel.

"Work with what you got, I always say!"

"Uh-huh," Jordan smirked at him. "Well now you've got a shovel, so work with that. What shall I do?"

"Bring me some tea, if ya got it."

"You have got to be kidding, you don't plan to let me help at all do you!" Jordan wished she was more surprised at his stubbornness, but in truth he had a tendency to play the 'knight in shining armor part,' as her mother liked to say.

He lingered in his digging to glance at her mischievously. "Oh tea would be a great help, I'm about as parched as these tomatoes. Besides," he checked his watch, "I'd say your mother will be here in about an hour with supper."

Jordan gawked. "You two are incorrigible!"

"I'm just saying you got time for a shower, if you want one. I know you and your momma can't stand to be dirty at the table."

Right again. Though she feigned frustration, but Jordan couldn't help but feel grateful for parents like hers. She knew too many in her social circle here and back in the city that couldn't say the same.

Giving in, she asked "You want lemon?"

"As long as you didn't grow it."

"Oh hush!"

Jordan could hear her father's guffaws all the way up the back porch as she made her way into the kitchen to prepare him a glass. If nothing else, she'd just made tea that morning and with an hour's worth before her mother arrived she had time for a quick shower, to clear the table, and maybe even to put a batch of cookies in the oven.

When she reached the garden again her father had one railroad tie sticking up from a decent size hole in the ground and he was working to stabilize it with a few cinderblocks and more dirt. She handed him the glass.

"Thanks, doll," he sipped his tea, eyeing her.

"What?"

"Well, I'm here working on your...shall we say *unique* garden, and I can't help but notice something."

Jordan looked around. "The gravestones are missing?"

Her father shook his head, his shaggy blonde hair dripping sweat beads in the places where it stuck out from his hat. "I see about 10 dying or dead tomato plants and not a single other crop."

Jordan dropped her head at once, idly wringing her hands. "Well... I just haven't planted anything else yet. I've been too busy fighting with the tomatoes."

"But Jo, you don't even like tomatoes," her father stated incredulously.

"Lots of people grow crops they don't like..."

"Jo." His tone was growing stern. He knew she was keeping something from him, but the whole thing just seemed so silly she didn't want to admit it. She hadn't even told her mother.

Finally unable to take his scrutiny any longer, she confessed, "Alex likes tomatoes. Specifically fried green tomatoes. I thought if I could make some to take over..." she trailed off, too embarrassed to continue. She put a hand over her face. "I know its dumb."

Her father started to respond, but suddenly he was overcome with giggles and couldn't speak.

"See! You think its dumb too!" She turned away. Her face was redder than even a sunburn could make it.

"Aw honey, I don't think it's dumb." She felt his hand rub her shoulders. "I think you're just cute as a button." He paused and pulled his phone from the holster on his hip.

What a dork.

"You know, I'd be willing to bet your mom would be thrilled to make some fried green tomatoes for tonight. It'd even take her a bit of extra time so you'd have more opportunity to fuss over the house." He winked at her, a knowing, tickled look he had long ago perfected. "Why don't you invite Alex to dinner?"

Jordan chewed her lip as she thought about his suggestion. She *had* promised to invite Alex over after they'd closed on the house. Afterall, it was Alex's grandparents' house and Alex who had helped sell Jordan the property. She was just nervous.

Sensing her hesitation, her father whispered, "We don't have to tell her about the cemetery...oh I mean garden." He put on his best impression of her and the joke was successful. Jordan's lips formed a small smile. She nodded.

"Great! Now get on up to the house, wouldn't want you to miss out on the on all the fussin'. I'll call your mother."

Jordan took off to the back porch and flew through her house like a hurricane, all the stuff she needed to straighten up flooding her mind at once. She was just about to hop in the shower by the time she realized she hadn't even texted Alex yet. With shaky fingers she typed out: *Come to dinner?* and pressed send before she realized how that might come across as a bit rude. Quickly she followed up with: *Please? At 6:30.* And for good measure she threw in: *We're having fried green tomatoes.*

She put her phone face down on the vanity, too nervous to wait for a response, and popped under the hot water for the quickest shower of her life.

When she got out she had no choice but to look at her phone at last. Alex had responded: *Sounds delicious. I'll be there.*

Jordan was so giddy she threw her clothes on with lightning speed and bounced out onto the porch. Her father looked up at the stuttered smack of the screen door in its frame.

"Well?" he shouted.

"She'll be here!" Jordan was pretty sure she screeched more than necessary, but her father didn't seem to mind.

"Congratulations, pumpkin! Your momma is on her way, she said she'd cook here and help you straighten up," she watched as he started to go back to his work digging another hole opposite the first, but suddenly he looked back to her. "You might wanna put your shirt on the right way," he chuckled.

Jordan glanced down to see the back side of her shirt staring up at her. *Whoopsie.* She was already putting her arms in her sleeves to twist it around as she turned to go back in the house.

"Thanks Dad!" she called over her shoulder.

In the garden her father smiled to himself. He'd been worried when Jordan moved home that it would be harder for her to find happiness in their small town, but suddenly he was feeling all the better. He'd get this garden going, he was certain. If Jordan wanted to give fried green tomatoes to Alex, he was going to help make it happen.

Wisteria Blooms and a Hint of Cotillion

Susan Dickenson

Maggie Stillwell was stuck. Stuck in traffic for the umpteenth time and stuck in life. *I'm so sick of all this pavement*, she thought. A blast of the horn from the car beside her punctuated her thoughts. "And gas fumes and concrete and rude people," she muttered. It was only Wednesday. The weekend seemed too far away for any comfort. Even the landscape along the interstate seemed to conspire against her. "Everything is bleak and grey and lifeless," she grumbled.

She found herself tapping the steering wheel and absentmindedly humming along to a song on the radio. The lyrics' symbolism of taking the long way to get to the end of one's journey spoke directly to her heart.

"Home," she chuckled. "I need to go home." The epiphany surprised her.

An hour and a half, and twenty-five miles later, she reflexively pressed her garage door opener, eased her car into the garage, and thrust the shifter into park. She clenched the steering wheel of her posh car parked in the garage of her posh home. *I have a house but is it really my home?* Maggie pondered. She grudgingly got out of the car and made her way to the door separating the garage and her modern deco kitchen. She grimaced at the "Live, Laugh, Love" sign over the doorway, unlocked the door, and went into the kitchen. After placing her handbag and laptop case on the counter, she pressed her hands onto the surface beside them. *Cold, hard granite,* she mused. *That's how I feel these days.*

The ring of her home phone roused her from her ruminations. She answered without looking at the caller id. "Hello," she said glumly.

"Maggie? It's Mom. You sound tired, honey. What's wrong?" Her mother, Naomi, had a keen sixth sense which was credited to "being raised in the mountains and taught the old ways." She always phoned just when she was needed.

"Oh, it was a long commute this afternoon. I actually just got home," Maggie explained. "Mom, do you have plans for the weekend?" she asked.

"Nothing that can't be changed," Naomi replied. "Are you coming home?"

"I think I just might, well, if I can get free of Friday's schedule," Maggie clarified. "I have a meeting, but I think I can postpone it a week."

"Call me when you're on your way, honey, and be safe. Love you."

"I will, Mom. Love you, too."

Maggie returned the phone to the charging base, walked to the other side of her expansive gourmet kitchen—which she rarely used—and retrieved a bottle of red wine. "Alexa," she called out. "Play *Fleetwood Mac* playlist." The familiar guitar prelude of *Rhiannon* began to play as Maggie poured herself a large glass of cab. She started to place the bottle on the counter but shrugged her shoulders and walked to the connecting sunroom, bottle and glass in hand. As she sat down on her floral-patterned settee, the theme of the song caught her attention. It conveyed the character of a woman who was formidable, a woman who clearly had a grasp of her own worth and self-determination.

"When did I stop flying?" Maggie wondered aloud as she stared at the lifeless flowerbeds in her backyard.

* * *

"I'll be back in the office on Monday," Maggie assured her client as she drove toward the mountains of her childhood. "We can do lunch or an early supper if you like." The cell phone signal began to cut in and out, garbling her client's reply. "I'm on a stretch of road with low signal," she interjected. "I'll email you later this weekend to confirm for Monday. See you soon," she concluded and pressed the 'End' button on her car's navigation screen.

Maggie exhaled a long sigh as she topped the hill on Route 460 that lead down to the stretch of road her family nicknamed *Gasoline Valley*. Cell phone signal was spotty at best, ensuring she would not receive any more calls for at least thirty minutes. *A nice respite*, she thought. Soon she would top another hill where the peak of Brush Mountain first comes into view. She was tempted to take the Blue Ridge Parkway exit so she could meander along the winding road and think about her life, but the call of the hills of Holston Mountain was stronger, so she drove on through Cloverdale to Interstate 81. Her lips spread into a lop-sided grin. *Another couple of hours, and I'll be home.*

The drive along I-81 was a little more hectic than Maggie would have liked, but she ticked off the time by the exits she passed. Christiansburg, Wytheville, Marion, Chilhowie—and then the sign for the Abingdon exits. The last bit of tension in her neck eased as she took exit nineteen and headed toward her mother's home on the river off Alvarado Road.

As she turned down the gravel road which led to her mother's home, she noticed a 'For Sale' sign on the pebble stone drive of the Peterson's house. "That's odd," she puzzled aloud. "Mom didn't mention that Mammaw's old homeplace was up for sale." She would have to ask about that. The Petersons had purchased the homeplace from her Mammaw's estate when Maggie was in elementary school. Her mother knew she didn't like that it had passed out of the family and had always wished to buy it. Maggie frowned. *Maybe Mom assumed I wasn't interested any more since I moved away*, she thought as she pulled into the driveway.

"Ok," she said perplexed. "Another oddity." Naomi's car wasn't parked in the drive.

Maggie got out of her car and retrieved her weekend bag from the trunk. As she walked toward the porch, she noticed grape hyacinths and yellow, white, and lilac crocuses blooming wildly around the base of the dogwood on the front lawn. Her mother's yard seemed to always teem with life regardless of the season. As she climbed the porch steps she noticed a folded piece of peach-colored paper tucked in between the screen door and its frame. She placed her bag on the rocking chair nearest her and retrieved the note.

> *Maggie,*
> *Went into town to buy some of those scones and jam that you like. Should be back around the time you get here. Juniper will be by shortly and we'll sit in the sunroom and enjoy afternoon tea together. Key's where it always is.*
> *Love,*
> *Mom*

Maggie chuckled as she retrieved the key from under the flowerpot by the front door and let herself into the house. She was a little peckish and would enjoy a light meal. As she sat down to rest, she heard the front door open.

Juniper walked briskly into the den and plopped down on the couch. "Sooo, what brings you home, Mags?" she asked.

"Supertramp," Maggie replied.

"Come again?" Juniper asked.

"A song on the radio," Maggie replied sheepishly. "I was stuck in traffic on 95 and Supertramp was playing on the radio."

"Gotcha, I think." Juniper's head tilted to the side. "Who's Supertramp?"

Juniper was eight years younger than Maggie and wasn't a fan of seventies' music. Her musical tastes aligned with hip hop and cross-over country songs. Maggie had a more eclectic taste in music and enjoyed many genres.

"A British band from the seventies." Maggie grinned. "I'll play you a song some time. You've probably heard one, you just don't know their name. Hey, while I'm thinking about it, how long have the Petersons had the old homeplace up for sale?"

"Actually, not long," she responded. "They wanted to move to town. Mrs. Peterson is tired of the stairs and says she can't keep the place clean. Mr. Peterson said he's tired of keeping the lawn mowed." Juniper shrugged. "They bought a patio home on the golf course."

The sound of the front door opening caught their attention. "I guess Mom's home," Juniper said.

A familiar smell of perfume wafted through the air. Maggie's breath caught in her throat and her spine tingled. *Mammaw?* she thought.

"What perfume are you wearing, Mom?" Juniper asked as Naomi entered the room.

"I saw a vintage Siamese cat bottle of Cotillion online. I couldn't resist ordering it," she explained. "I thought of Mother and just wanted the bottle, but when it came, I opened it and it still smelled good."

"I'd forgotten what that smelled like," Maggie said. "I can't believe it still smells good after all these years."

"An ethereal surprise, Magnolia," Naomi avowed. "It came in the mail the same day the Petersons put their house up for sale."

"Mom," Juniper cringed. "I don't know what's worse–using Maggie's full name or supernatural talk."

Juniper was born after their Mammaw passed. She never had the opportunity to learn the old ways or hear the stories their Mammaw told so keenly.

"Honestly, Juniper, I don't mind," Maggie assured her sister.

"Well, I'm off," Juniper replied as she quickly rose from the couch.

"Aren't you staying for tea? We'll have a girls' afternoon," Naomi urged.

"Sorry, I promised Amanda I'd help her plan her sister's baby shower today," she explained. "I'll come by tomorrow for lunch, if that's okay."

"Well, be careful, honey," Naomi said. "We'll see you tomorrow."

"Later, Mags," Juniper said over her shoulder as she left.

"See you tomorrow," Maggie replied. Her sister could be a handful and was more free-spirited and had more in common with their Mammaw than she knew.

"Would you help me set the tea?" Naomi asked as she walked toward the kitchen, drawing Maggie's attention back to her hungry stomach.

"Oh, yes," she answered. "I've missed Miss Martha's scones. Thanks for going out to buy some, Mom."

"I thought we'd take some time to talk and enjoy the sunshine streaming into the sunroom. It's been so dreary this week. You must've brought the sun with you," Naomi quipped.

"I wouldn't say that. I've been pretty gloomy lately," Maggie confessed.

"Problems with work?" Naomi asked as she put the kettle on for tea.

"Not necessarily problems, just life in general. I feel sort of unfulfilled, which is ridiculous because I have so much," she confided.

"Well, let's take this tray of goodies into the sunroom and you can tell me all about it," Naomi encouraged.

* * *

The weekend went by all too quickly. It was Monday morning and Maggie was sitting at her desk—back to her weekly routine. A forty-five-minute commute, two-minute walk to the office, and all the phone calls she could make. Her mother's wise words kept interrupting her thoughts. "Having nice things doesn't always equal fulfillment. A life worth living isn't built on what you can touch, Magnolia. It's the smell of wisteria on a fresh spring day. The soothing sound of wind chimes caressed by a cool summer breeze. You've forgotten your roots, honey. But they're right here, always waiting to nurture you."

Maggie rummaged through her desk drawer and found the business card a realtor had mailed to her. It was only a few weeks ago that a woman cold-called to inquire about the possibility of Maggie selling her home to a potential buyer who was moving to the city. Maggie had originally scoffed at the idea, but she couldn't get the image of her Mammaw's homeplace out of her mind. She could sell her home for a tidy profit and buy the old homeplace with money to spare. She stared at the business card. It sounded easy enough, though she would need a new job and she would have to let this job go.

I must be crazy, she thought. *How do I give up a job that pays what this one pays?* And then another epiphany surprised her. *Because I miss the smell of wisteria, the gentle lull of the river, and the green hills of home.*

Maggie picked up her cellphone and called the realtor.

* * *

Juniper observed her sister as they sat on the porch swing of their Mammaw's homeplace. The soft sway of the swing was soothing and created a sense of contentment that she hadn't felt in quite a while.

"I never thought you'd ever move back here," Juniper quipped. "But I did miss you a lot."

"I never thought I'd move back either," Maggie admitted.

"Well, Mags, I'm off, but I'll come back by to finish helping you clean and unpack tomorrow. You'd better not stay too long out here. It'll be cold as ice after the sun goes down," Juniper said.

"I won't. I think I'll finish off this cup of coffee and then head in for a shower," Maggie replied.

"Yeah, you're pretty grimy," Juniper said as she walked down the porch steps of their Mammaw's old homeplace.

"You don't smell so great yourself, Sis," Maggie retorted. "See you tomorrow, and Juniper—thanks."

"No problem," she replied with a backward wave.

Maggie surveyed the early blooming flowers scattered around the limestone boulders which dotted her yard. The river gently flowed just beyond the tree line. She watched the winter sun slowly disappear behind the ridge. She felt the warmth from its rays wane, replaced by crisp, frosty night air. In a few weeks spring would come, ushering in the lovely violet wisteria blooms she so desperately missed. A slight breeze jingled the windchimes hanging near her and a sudden waft of Cotillion filled the air. A smile spread across her face and filled her heart with promise. *Yes,* she thought. *I may have taken the long way, but it feels good to be back in Mammaw's wild mountain home.*

Tell Me Again

Linda Hudson Hoagland

"Please, Sylvia, give me a moment to think," said Mandy sharply.

"Why do you have to think? The answer is pretty obvious. There is nothing to think about," I said as I made no attempt to hide my sarcasm.

"If we are going to do something as reckless as killing someone, we really should discuss this a little more," Mandy said as she tried not to whine.

"Do you not think that he deserves killing?" I asked in a harsh whisper.

"Of course I do, Sylvia. You don't even have to ask me that question," replied Mandy.

"Okay then, let's get with it. We have to get this all figured out. I'm on a really tight schedule," I whispered.

"Tell me again about why we have to kill your husband. You told me he is abusive, but you can handle that simply by leaving him. So—why don't you?" asked Mandy.

"Why don't I what?"

"Leave him? That's the easiest way to get rid of an abusive husband," said Mandy.

"I have two little boys and I don't have a job. Where would I go? What would I do to make a living?" I asked.

"Do you have any family in the area?" asked Mandy.

"You know I don't have any family, Mandy."

"What about friends?" asked Mandy.

"Just you. He never allowed me to have friends. You know that, too," I said.

"What about women's shelters? There are some in the area, you know," said Mandy almost sarcastically.

"No, I don't think so. Your house it too small. I couldn't stay with you and it would be too dangerous anyway. It would be too close to him. I like my house. I like my lifestyle. I want him to have to pay for my way of living with his life insurance money," I whispered.

"That sounds really selfish, Sylvia,"

"I know, I know, but that's how I feel," I said.

"You are going to have to change that attitude. No one is going to have one bit of sympathy for you if you are caught," said Mandy.

"Okay, okay, how about that I'm a helpless mother who has never worked a day in her life and who has no idea of where to go for help. Remember, he has not allowed me to do anything without his permission. I wasn't even allowed to leave the house unless he was with me," I explained.

"How did you get out today?" asked Mandy.

"I drugged his coffee," I said.

"You're kidding," gasped Mandy.

"I wish I were."

"What about your boys? Where are they?" Mandy asked.

"With his mother. She wanted to play grandma today," I answered sullenly.

"You really had to drug him to get out of the house?" asked an astonished Mandy.

"Yes, is that so hard to believe?" I asked.

"How did you get the car keys?" Mandy asked.

"I called the dealership and asked for a duplicate because mine had been destroyed. Because of my name, my husband's name that is, they mailed me a new one. Of course, I never had a key. My husband wouldn't give me one, but the dealership was more than happy to replace my crushed key," I said with a smile.

"That's a sneaky and smart way to get a key," said Mandy.

"Well, it worked. I got my key or I wouldn't be talking to you now," I said with a grin.

"When are you—er we—going to have to do the deed?" asked Mandy,

"How about right now?" I said excitedly.

"How?" Mandy snapped.

"I want you to come to my house and my husband will have an awful accident," I said with a fake look of concern.

"How strong was that drug you gave him?" Mandy asked.

"Strong enough. He will sleep for a while. I really need you to help me get this done," I said as I pleaded with Mandy.

"Just tell me one thing," Mandy said.

"What's that?" I asked.

"All the times you have come to see me, did you have to drug him to leave the house?" Mandy asked.

"I haven't been able to see you very many times and you are my best friend. You are closer to me than a sister would be," I said.

"Did you drug him each time?" Mandy persisted.

"No, today was the first for the drugs. The other times a coworker or friend picked him up to take him somewhere. He didn't take the car and I had a key so I got to visit with you for a little while without him knowing about it. The last time I slipped out I think he had kept track of the mileage. He asked me if anyone had used the car. Of course, I said I didn't see anyone and I reminded him he never gave me a key. He just let it drop but I knew he was getting suspicious. I knew I couldn't sneak the car out anymore without being punished," I explained.

"What would he do to you? How would he punish you?" Mandy asked.

"Oh, you would never see the marks unless I was naked. He never hit any area of my body that would be exposed," I answered.

"Is he really that mean and cruel?" Mandy asked.

"I would show you, but the last beating has faded," I replied sadly. "Are you going to help me? We have to go real soon so we can get the deed done."

I took my car and Mandy drove her own vehicle because I wasn't going to be able to drive her back to her vehicle after the accident.

I pulled onto my driveway first and Mandy followed me. She needed to have her car parked for an easy escape. I didn't want her to be around when I found the body of my dead husband.

I climbed from my car, closing the door without slamming it. I motioned for Mandy to do the same.

It's funny how being sneaky makes you want to squat down and hide from unwanted eyes. I'm sure we looked comical but that wasn't the look I was wanting. I thought we needed to appear driven and focused.

I unlocked the back door to the kitchen and motioned for Mandy to follow me inside.

"We've got to be quiet," I whispered as we walked through the kitchen.

"I thought you said he was knocked out from the drugs," Mandy said skeptically.

"Yes, I hope so. I gave him enough to knock out an elephant," I said.

"Then why do we have to be so quiet?" Mandy asked.

"Just in case. That's all," I answered in a whisper.

The staircase to the second floor and foyer were just beyond the kitchen.

I crept slowly into the foyer and looked toward the staircase guiding my glance to the head of the steps.

It was clear; he wasn't standing there watching me sneak up to commit murder.

"Come on, Mandy. We need to go upstairs," I whispered.

I stood outside of the closed bedroom door. My next step would be to turn the knob and go inside.

Suddenly, I was afraid to move. I wanted to turn tail and run. My mind was racing, showing me the multitude of reasons for why I shouldn't be doing this.

"What's wrong?" whispered Mandy.

"Nothing, I was just listening for sounds of movement," I whispered.

I slowly turned the knob and opened the door.

He was gone!

My mouth dropped open as I stared at the empty bed.

"Where is he?" whispered Mandy.

"I don't know," I answered as I continued to look around the empty room.

"What now?" Mandy asked.

"I've got to find him. I hope he isn't mad at me for using the car. I hope and pray he doesn't know that I have a key," I said with apprehension.

"What does that matter? You are planning to kill him and he can't get mad at you if you do that," said a confused Mandy.

The bathroom door was standing open so I knew he wasn't hiding in there.

"Let's go back downstairs. I need to find him," I told Mandy,

I walked into the living room and he was sitting on his easy chair watching the both of us.

"Are you finished yet?" he asked.

"What are you talking about? Finished with what?" I asked as I looked annoyed.

"Planning my death, like you did last month," he said.

"No, no, that's not what we're doing," I sputtered.

"Yes, it is and it's not going to work," he said with a haughty laugh.

"Why not?" I asked loudly.

"I know what you're doing, Sylvia. Does your friend know?" he asked with a smirk.

"No," I snapped.

"Don't you think you should tell her?" he asked.

"What is he talking about, Sylvia?" Mandy demanded.

"It's a game we play. Arnie and me. Oh, by the way, this fine, handsome man is my husband of ten years. I'm a writer and this is how I devise my murders," I explained.

"How could you do this to me?" demanded Mandy.

"It's the best way for me to put reality into my stories," I explained softly.

"Reality? I was going to help you kill someone! Is that real enough for you?" Mandy screamed.

"Please, Mandy, it was just a way for me to get help with my story," I explained.

"I was going to help you kill your husband and it was fodder for your book. I'm getting out of here, Sylvia. Please don't ever call me again," Mandy screamed as she stomped out the door.

"How many *best* friends have you lost now, Sylvia?" asked Arnie.

"About ten but it's the best way I have found for role-playing my book ideas," I explained. "I hope Mandy can forgive me but if not, that's okay, too. I'll find another friend, just like I found her," I said with a grin.

"You're heartless, Sylvia," said Arnie with a broad smile.

"No, I'm not. It's just a game with me and I like to do it. As long as I still have you, I will never be alone," I said as I hugged his neck pulling him up close.

"One day, Sylvia, someone is going to get mad enough to kill you. You know that, don't you?" Arnie said.

"Maybe," I said as we walked toward the bedroom. "If that happens, you can write the book."

About the Authors

Lori C. Byington lives in Bristol, Tennessee with her husband, son and two dogs. She is a Professor of Composition at King University in Bristol, TN, a graduate of King College (1985) and ETSU (1987), and her short stories have been published in several previous anthologies from Jan-Carol Publishing, Inc.

Susan Dickenson was born in Richmond, Virginia, but spent her childhood summers in Northeast Tennessee where she met and married her high school sweetheart. After living in Washington, Germany, and Texas, they moved to the beautiful foothills of Southwest Virginia. Dickenson enjoys spending time with her family, birding, and writing. She is currently working on her debut novel.

Lynda A. Holmes is a lifelong Georgia resident, retired educator, and author. Her publications include professional articles, poetry, memoirs; southern fiction, and historical fiction (*Mineral Spirits*, Jan-Carol Publishing, Inc. 2015). She won the American Heritage National First Place Awards for Drama and Poetry from the National Society Daughters of the American Revolution.

Jan Howery, a native of Southwest Virginia, writes with an Appalachian influence. Her many writings include "The Daisy Flower Garden," featured in the anthology *Broken Petals*, and "The Devil Behind the Barn" featured in the anthology *These Haunted Hills: A Collection of Short Stories*, "The Straight Back Chair," in *These Haunted Hills Book 2*, "Right or Wrong," featured in *Wild Daisies*, and "The Love of Daisies" in *Scattered Flowers*. Other writings include fashion and health columns for the Appalachian regional magazine for women, *Voice Magazine for Women*.

Linda Hudson Hoagland from Tazewell, Virginia, has written many mystery novels along with works of nonfiction, four collections of short writings and four volumes of poems. Mysteries and short stories are her favorite pastime and she has won many awards as well as being published.

George Justice holds a B.A. in English Literature. He has been published five times for short stories, three times for poetry, and was a longtime movie critic for Michigan's *Oakland County Tribune*. As a veteran, he wrote numerous articles (from human interest to military) for *Stars and Stripes*. His first novel *Greezy Creek* was published in September 2019.

Draco Sage has studied numerous forms of writing, but enjoys most playwriting, poetry, and romantic fiction. A Middle Tennessee resident, their home library boasts over 600 books and an incredibly comfortable rocking chair. When not reading or writing—for either business or pleasure—you can find Sage enjoying tabletop RPGs with family and friends.

Rebecca Williams Spindler is an award-winning author, screenwriter, producer, and mom. She writes female-driven stories with humor and heart. As an Asian-Appalachian American, Rebecca's diverse family fuels her content. She's taught writing at the college level and presented workshops at book festivals and writer's conferences. She is also Co-Host of a podcast for emerging writers, "Faith, Final Drafts and the F-Word." (We keep it PG-13.) www.spindlerwriting.com

LOOK FOR OUR OTHER SHORT-STORY COLLECTIONS:

"every story needs a book"

LITTLE CREEK BOOKS
MOUNTAIN GIRL PRESS
EXPRESS EDITIONS
ROSEHEART
BROKEN CROW RIDGE
FIERY NIGHT
SKIPPY CREEK

JanCarolPublishing.com

CPSIA information can be obtained
at www.ICGtesting.com
Printed in the USA
BVHW071112200922
647490BV00003B/444

9 781954 978546